W9-BJU-860

WITHDRAWN

SHORT CRUISES

SHORT CRUISES

BY

W. W. JACOBS

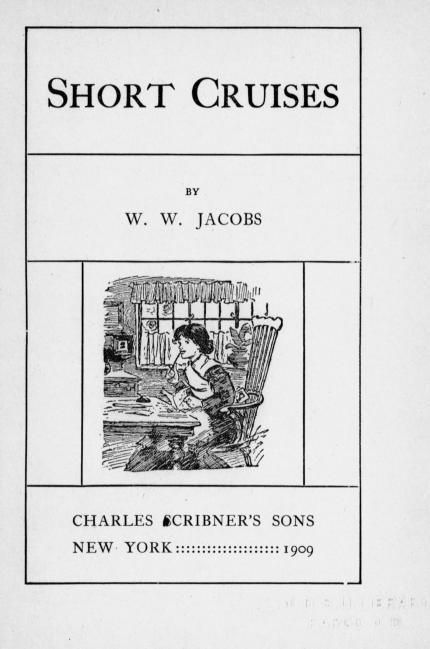

CHARLES SCRIBNER'S SONS
NEW YORK ::::::::::::::::: 1909

N. D. S. U. LIBRARY
FARGO N. D.

COPYRIGHT, 1906, 1907, BY

W. W. JACOBS

COPYRIGHT, 1907, BY

CHARLES SCRIBNER'S SONS

All rights reserved

Published, April, 1907

PR
4821
J2
S5

N.D.S.U. LIBRARY
FARGO N.D.

CONTENTS

74603

ILLUSTRATIONS

FROM DRAWINGS BY WILL OWEN

vii

Illustrations

viii

THE CHANGELING

The Changeling

MR. GEORGE HENSHAW let himself in at the front door, and stood for some time wiping his boots on the mat. The little house was ominously still, and a faint feeling, only partially due to the lapse of time since breakfast, manifested itself behind his waistcoat. He coughed—a matter-of-fact cough—and, with an attempt to hum a tune, hung his hat on the peg and entered the kitchen.

Mrs. Henshaw had just finished dinner. The neatly cleaned bone of a chop was on a plate by her side; a small dish which had contained a rice-pudding was empty; and the only food left on the table was a small rind of cheese and a piece of stale bread. Mr. Henshaw's face fell, but he drew his chair up to the table and waited.

His wife regarded him with a fixed and offensive stare. Her face was red and her eyes were blazing. It was hard to ignore her gaze; harder still to meet it. Mr. Henshaw, steering a middle course, allowed

3

The Changeling

his eyes to wander round the room and to dwell, for the fraction of a second, on her angry face.

"You've had dinner early?" he said at last, in a trembling voice.

"Have I?" was the reply.

Mr. Henshaw sought for a comforting explanation. "Clock's fast," he said, rising and adjusting it.

His wife rose almost at the same moment, and with slow deliberate movements began to clear the table.

"What—what about dinner?" said Mr. Henshaw, still trying to control his fears.

"Dinner!" repeated Mrs. Henshaw, in a terrible voice. "You go and tell that creature you were on the 'bus with to get your dinner."

Mr. Henshaw made a gesture of despair. "I tell you," he said emphatically, "it wasn't me. I told you so last night. You get an idea in your head and——"

"That'll do," said his wife, sharply. "I saw you, George Henshaw, as plain as I see you now. You were tickling her ear with a bit o' straw, and that good-for-nothing friend of yours, Ted Stokes, was sitting behind with another beauty. Nice way o' going on, and me at 'ome all alone by myself, slaving and slaving to keep things respectable!"

4

The Changeling

"It wasn't me," reiterated the unfortunate.

"When I called out to you," pursued the unheeding Mrs. Henshaw, "you started and pulled your hat over your eyes and turned away. I should have caught you if it hadn't been for all them carts in the way and falling down. I can't understand now how it was I wasn't killed; I was a mask of mud from head to foot."

Despite his utmost efforts to prevent it, a faint smile flitted across the pallid features of Mr. Henshaw.

"Yes, you may laugh," stormed his wife, "and I've no doubt them two beauties laughed too. I'll take care you don't have much more to laugh at, my man."

She flung out of the room and began to wash up the crockery. Mr. Henshaw, after standing irresolute for some time with his hands in his pockets, put on his hat again and left the house.

He dined badly at a small eating-house, and returned home at six o'clock that evening to find his wife out and the cupboard empty. He went back to the same restaurant for tea, and after a gloomy meal went round to discuss the situation with Ted Stokes. That gentleman's suggestion of a double alibi he thrust aside with disdain and a stern appeal to talk sense.

The Changeling

"Mind, if my wife speaks to you about it," he said, warningly, "it wasn't me, but somebody like me. You might say he 'ad been mistook for me before."

Mr. Stokes grinned and, meeting a freezing glance from his friend, at once became serious again.

"Why not say it was you?" he said stoutly. "There's no harm in going for a 'bus-ride with a friend and a couple o' ladies."

"O' course there ain't," said the other, hotly, "else I shouldn't ha' done it. But you know what my wife is."

Mr. Stokes, who was by no means a favorite of the lady in question, nodded. "You *were* a bit larky, too," he said thoughtfully. "You 'ad quite a little slapping game after you pretended to steal her brooch."

"I s'pose when a gentleman's with a lady he 'as got to make 'imself pleasant?" said Mr. Henshaw, with dignity. "Now, if my missis speaks to you about it, you say that it wasn't me, but a friend of yours up from the country who is as like me as two peas. See?"

"Name o' Dodd," said Mr. Stokes, with a knowing nod. "Tommy Dodd."

"I'm not playing the giddy goat," said the other, bitterly, "and I'd thank you not to."

6

The Changeling

"All right," said Mr. Stokes, somewhat taken aback. "Any name you like; I don't mind."

Mr. Henshaw pondered. "Any sensible name'll do," he said, stiffly.

"Bell?" suggested Mr. Stokes. "Alfred Bell? I did know a man o' that name once. He tried to borrow a bob off of me."

"That'll do," said his friend, after some consideration; "but mind you stick to the same name. And you'd better make up something about him—where he lives, and all that sort of thing—so that you can stand being questioned without looking more like a silly fool than you can help."

"I'll do what I can for you," said Mr. Stokes, "but I don't s'pose your missis'll come to me at all. She saw you plain enough."

They walked on in silence and, still deep in thought over the matter, turned into a neighboring tavern for refreshment. Mr. Henshaw drank his with the air of a man performing a duty to his constitution; but Mr. Stokes, smacking his lips, waxed eloquent over the brew.

"I hardly know what I'm drinking," said his friend, forlornly. "I suppose it's four-half, because that's what I asked for."

Mr. Stokes gazed at him in deep sympathy. "It can't be so bad as that," he said, with concern.

The Changeling

"You wait till you're married," said Mr. Henshaw, brusquely. "You'd no business to ask me to go with you, and I was a good-natured fool to do it."

"You stick to your tale and it'll be all right," said the other. "Tell her that you spoke to me about it, and that his name is Alfred Bell—B E double L—and that he lives in—in Ireland. Here! I say!"

"Well," said Mr. Henshaw, shaking off the hand which the other had laid on his arm.

"You—you be Alfred Bell," said Mr. Stokes, breathlessly.

Mr. Henshaw started and eyed him nervously. His friend's eyes were bright and, he fancied, a bit wild.

"Be Alfred Bell," repeated Mr. Stokes. "Don't you see? Pretend to be Alfred Bell and go with me to your missis. I'll lend you a suit o' clothes and a fresh neck-tie, and there you are."

"*What?*" roared the astounded Mr. Henshaw.

"It's as easy as easy," declared the other. "To-morrow evening, in a new rig-out, I walks you up to your house and asks for you to show you to yourself. Of course, I'm sorry you ain't in, and perhaps we walks in to wait for you."

"Show me to myself?" gasped Mr. Henshaw.

Mr. Stokes winked. "On account o' the surpris-

8

ing likeness," he said, smiling. " It is surprising, ain't it? Fancy the two of us sitting there and talking to her and waiting for you to come in and wondering what's making you so late ! "

Mr. Henshaw regarded him steadfastly for some seconds, and then, taking a firm hold of his mug, slowly drained the contents.

" And what about my voice? " he demanded, with something approaching a sneer.

" That's right," said Mr. Stokes, hotly; " it wouldn't be you if you didn't try to make difficulties."

" But what about it? " said Mr. Henshaw, obstinately.

" You can alter it, can't you? " said the other.

They were alone in the bar, and Mr. Henshaw, after some persuasion, was induced to try a few experiments. He ranged from bass, which hurt his throat, to a falsetto which put Mr. Stokes's teeth on edge, but in vain. The rehearsal was stopped at last by the landlord, who, having twice come into the bar under the impression that fresh customers had entered, spoke his mind at some length. " Seem to think you're in a blessed monkey-house," he concluded, severely.

" We thought we was," said Mr. Stokes, with a long appraising sniff, as he opened the door. " It's a mistake anybody might make."

The Changeling

He pushed Mr. Henshaw into the street as the landlord placed a hand on the flap of the bar, and followed him out.

" You'll have to 'ave a bad cold and talk in 'usky whispers," he said slowly, as they walked along. " You caught a cold travelling in the train from Ireland day before yesterday, and you made it worse going for a ride on the outside of a 'bus with me and a couple o' ladies. See? Try 'usky whispers now."

Mr. Henshaw tried, and his friend, observing that he was taking but a languid interest in the scheme, was loud in his praises. " I should never 'ave known you," he declared. " Why, it's wonderful! Why didn't you tell me you could act like that? "

Mr. Henshaw remarked modestly that he had not been aware of it himself, and, taking a more hopefu' view of the situation, whispered himself into such a state of hoarseness that another visit for refreshment became absolutely necessary.

" Keep your 'art up and practise," said Mr. Stokes, as he shook hands with him some time later. " And if you can manage it, get off at four o'clock to-morrow and we'll go round to see her while she thinks you're still at work."

Mr. Henshaw complimented him upon his artful-

The Changeling

" ' And what about my voice ? ' he demanded."

ness, and, with some confidence in a man of such resource, walked home in a more cheerful frame of mind. His heart sank as he reached the house, but to his relief the lights were out and his wife was in bed.

He was up early next morning, but his wife showed no signs of rising. The cupboard was still empty, and for some time he moved about hungry and undecided. Finally he mounted the stairs again, and with a view to arranging matters for the evening remonstrated with her upon her behavior and loudly announced his intention of not coming home until she was in a better frame of mind. From a disciplinary point of view the effect of the remonstrance was somewhat lost by being shouted through the closed door, and he also broke off too abruptly when Mrs. Henshaw opened it suddenly and confronted him. Fragments of the peroration reached her through the front door.

Despite the fact that he left two hours earlier, the day passed but slowly, and he was in a very despondent state of mind by the time he reached Mr. Stokes's lodging. The latter, however, had cheerfulness enough for both, and, after helping his visitor to change into fresh clothes and part his hair in the middle instead of at the side, surveyed him with grinning satisfaction. Under his directions Mr. Hen-

The Changeling

shaw also darkened his eyebrows and beard with a little burnt cork until Mr. Stokes declared that his own mother wouldn't know him.

"Now, be careful," said Mr. Stokes, as they set off. "Be bright and cheerful; be a sort o' ladies' man to her, same as she saw you with the one on the 'bus. Be as unlike yourself as you can, and don't forget yourself and call her by 'er pet name."

"Pet name!" said Mr. Henshaw, indignantly.

"Pet name! You'll alter your ideas of married life when you're caught, my lad, I can tell you!"

He walked on in scornful silence, lagging farther and farther behind as they neared his house. When Mr. Stokes knocked at the door he stood modestly aside with his back against the wall of the next house.

"Is George in?" inquired Mr. Stokes, carelessly, as Mrs. Henshaw opened the door.

"No," was the reply.

Mr. Stokes affected to ponder; Mr. Henshaw instinctively edged away.

"He ain't in," said Mrs. Henshaw, preparing to close the door.

"I wanted to see 'im partikler," said Mr. Stokes, slowly. "I brought a friend o' mine, name o' Alfred Bell, up here on purpose to see 'im."

Mrs. Henshaw, following the direction of his eyes, put her head round the door.

13

The Changeling

"George!" she exclaimed, sharply.

Mr. Stokes smiled. "That ain't George," he said, gleefully; "That's my friend, Mr. Alfred Bell. Ain't it a extraordinary likeness? Ain't it wonderful? That's why I brought 'im up; I wanted George to see 'im."

Mrs. Henshaw looked from one to the other in wrathful bewilderment.

"His living image, ain't he?" said Mr. Stokes. "This is my pal George's missis," he added, turning to Mr. Bell.

"Good afternoon to you," said that gentleman, huskily.

"He got a bad cold coming from Ireland," explained Mr. Stokes, "and, foolish-like, he went outside a 'bus with me the other night and made it worse."

"Oh-h!" said Mrs. Henshaw, slowly. "Indeed! Really!"

"He's quite curious to see George," said Mr. Stokes. "In fact, he was going back to Ireland tonight if it 'adn't been for that. He's waiting till to-morrow just to see George."

Mr. Bell, in a voice huskier than ever, said that he had altered his mind again.

"Nonsense!" said Mr. Stokes, sternly. "Besides, George would like to see you. I s'pose he

The Changeling

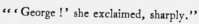

"'George!' she exclaimed, sharply."

won't be long?" he added, turning to Mrs. Henshaw, who was regarding Mr. Bell much as a hungry cat regards a plump sparrow.

" I don't suppose so," she said, slowly.

" I dare say if we wait a little while——" began Mr. Stokes, ignoring a frantic glance from Mr. Henshaw.

" Come in," said Mrs. Henshaw, suddenly.

Mr. Stokes entered and, finding that his friend hung back, went out again and half led, half pushed him indoors. Mr. Bell's shyness he attributed to his having lived so long in Ireland.

" He is quite the ladies' man, though," he said, artfully, as they followed their hostess into the front room. " You should ha' seen 'im the other night on the 'bus. We had a couple o' lady friends o' mine with us, and even the conductor was surprised at his goings on."

Mr. Bell, by no means easy as to the results of the experiment, scowled at him despairingly.

" Carrying on, was he?" said Mrs. Henshaw, regarding the culprit steadily.

" Carrying on like one o'clock," said the imaginative Mr. Stokes. " Called one of 'em his little wife, and asked her where 'er wedding-ring was."

" I didn't," said Mr. Bell, in a suffocating voice. " I didn't."

The Changeling

"There's nothing to be ashamed of," said Mr. Stokes, virtuously. "Only, as I said to you at the time, 'Alfred,' I says, 'it's all right for you as a single man, but you might be the twin-brother of a pal o' mine—George Henshaw by name—and if some people was to see you they might think it was 'im.' Didn't I say that?"

"You did," said Mr. Bell, helplessly.

"And he wouldn't believe me," said Mr. Stokes, turning to Mrs. Henshaw. "That's why I brought him round to see George."

"I should like to see the two of 'em together myself," said Mrs. Henshaw, quietly. "I should have taken him for my husband anywhere."

"You wouldn't if you'd seen 'im last night," said Mr. Stokes, shaking his head and smiling.

"Carrying on again, was he?" inquired Mrs. Henshaw, quickly.

"No!" said Mr. Bell, in a stentorian whisper.

His glance was so fierce that Mr. Stokes almost quailed. "I won't tell tales out of school," he said, nodding.

"Not if I ask you to?" said Mrs. Henshaw, with a winning smile.

"Ask 'im," said Mr. Stokes.

"Last night," said the whisperer, hastily, "I went for a quiet walk round Victoria Park all by myself.

17

The Changeling

Then I met Mr. Stokes, and we had one half-pint together at a public-house. That's all."

Mrs. Henshaw looked at Mr. Stokes. Mr. Stokes winked at her.

" It's as true as my name is—Alfred Bell," said that gentleman, with slight but natural hesitation.

" Have it your own way," said Mr. Stokes, somewhat perturbed at Mr. Bell's refusal to live up to the character he had arranged for him.

" I wish my husband spent his evenings in the same quiet way," said Mrs. Henshaw, shaking her head.

" Don't he?" said Mr. Stokes. " Why, he always seems quiet enough to me. Too quiet, I should say. Why, I never knew a quieter man. I chaff 'im about it sometimes."

" That's his artfulness," said Mrs. Henshaw.

" Always in a hurry to get 'ome," pursued the benevolent Mr. Stokes.

" He may say so to you to get away from you," said Mrs. Henshaw, thoughtfully. " He does say you're hard to shake off sometimes."

Mr. Stokes sat stiffly upright and threw a fierce glance in the direction of Mr. Henshaw.

" Pity he didn't tell me," he said bitterly. " I ain't one to force my company where it ain't wanted."

" I've said to him sometimes," continued Mrs. Henshaw, " ' Why don't you tell Ted Stokes plain

18

The Changeling

that you don't like his company?' but he won't.
That ain't his way. He'd sooner talk of you behind
your back."

"What does he say?" inquired Mr. Stokes, coldly
ignoring a frantic headshake on the part of his friend.

"Promise me you won't tell him if I tell you,"
said Mrs. Henshaw.

Mr. Stokes promised.

"I don't know that I ought to tell you," said
Mrs. Henshaw, reluctantly, "but I get so sick and
tired of him coming home and grumbling about
you."

"Go on," said the waiting Stokes.

Mrs. Henshaw stole a glance at him. "He says
you act as if you thought yourself everybody," she
said, softly, "and your everlasting clack, clack,
clack, worries him to death."

"Go on," said the listener, grimly.

"And he says it's so much trouble to get you to
pay for your share of the drinks that he'd sooner pay
himself and have done with it."

Mr. Stokes sprang from his chair and, with
clenched fists, stood angrily regarding the horrified
Mr. Bell. He composed himself by an effort and resumed his seat.

"Anything else?" he inquired.

"Heaps and heaps of things," said Mrs. Henshaw; "but I don't want to make bad blood between you."

"Don't mind me," said Mr. Stokes, glancing balefully over at his agitated friend. "P'raps I'll tell you some things about him some day."

"It would be only fair," said Mrs. Henshaw, quickly. "Tell me now; I don't mind Mr. Bell hearing; not a bit."

Mr. Bell spoke up for himself. "I don't want to hear family secrets," he whispered, with an imploring glance at. the vindictive Mr. Stokes. "It wouldn't be right."

"Well, *I* don't want to say things behind a man's back," said the latter, recovering himself. "Let's wait till George comes in, and I'll say 'em before his face."

Mrs. Henshaw, biting her lip with annoyance, argued with him, but in vain. Mr. Stokes was firm, and, with a glance at the clock, said that George would be in soon and he would wait till he came.

Conversation flagged despite the efforts of Mrs. Henshaw to draw Mr. Bell out on the subject of Ireland. At an early stage of the catechism he lost his voice entirely, and thereafter sat silent while Mrs. Henshaw discussed the most intimate affairs of her husband's family with Mr. Stokes. She was in the middle of an anecdote about her mother-in-law when

The Changeling

Mr. Bell rose and, with some difficulty, intimated his desire to depart.

"What, without seeing George?" said Mrs. Henshaw. "He can't be long now, and I should like to see you together."

"P'r'aps we shall meet him," said Mr. Stokes, who was getting rather tired of the affair. "Good night."

He led the way to the door and, followed by the eager Mr. Bell, passed out into the street. The knowledge that Mrs. Henshaw was watching him from the door kept him silent until they had turned the corner, and then, turning fiercely on Mr. Henshaw, he demanded to know what he meant by it.

"I've done with you," he said, waving aside the other's denials. "I've got you out of this mess, and now I've done with you. It's no good talking, because I don't want to hear it."

"Good-by, then," said Mr. Henshaw, with unexpected hauteur, as he came to a standstill.

"I'll 'ave my trousers first, though," said Mr. Stokes, coldly, "and then you can go, and welcome."

"It's my opinion she recognized me, and said all that just to try us," said the other, gloomily.

Mr. Stokes scorned to reply, and reaching his lodging stood by in silence while the other changed his clothes. He refused Mr. Henshaw's hand with a

21

gesture he had once seen on the stage, and, showing him downstairs, closed the door behind him with a bang.

Left to himself, the small remnants of Mr. Henshaw's courage disappeared. He wandered forlornly up and down the streets until past ten o'clock, and then, cold and dispirited, set off in the direction of home. At the corner of the street he pulled himself together by a great effort, and walking rapidly to his house put the key in the lock and turned it.

The door was fast and the lights were out. He knocked, at first lightly, but gradually increasing in loudness. At the fourth knock a light appeared in the room above, the window was raised, and Mrs. Henshaw leaned out.

"*Mr. Bell!*" she said, in tones of severe surprise.

"*Bell?*" said her husband, in a more surprised voice still. "It's me, Polly."

"Go away at once, sir!" said Mrs. Henshaw, indignantly. "How dare you call me by my Christian name? I'm surprised at you!"

"It's me, I tell you—George!" said her husband, desperately. "What do you mean by calling me Bell?"

"If you're Mr. Bell, as I suppose, you know well enough," said Mrs. Henshaw, leaning out and re-

The Changeling

"He struck a match and, holding it before his face, looked up at
the window."

garding him fixedly; "and if you're George **you** don't."

"I'm George," said Mr. Henshaw, hastily.

"I'm sure I don't know what to make of it," said Mrs. Henshaw, with a bewildered air. "Ted Stokes brought round a man named Bell this afternoon so like you that I can't tell the difference. I don't know what to do, but I do know this—I don't let you in until I have seen you both together, so that I can tell which is which."

"Both together!" exclaimed the startled Mr. Henshaw. "Here—look here!"

He struck a match and, holding it before his face, looked up at the window. Mrs. Henshaw scrutinized him gravely.

"It's no good," she said, despairingly. "I can't tell. I must see you both together."

Mr. Henshaw ground his teeth. "But where is he?" he inquired.

"He went off with Ted Stokes," said his wife. "If you're George you'd better go and ask him."

She prepared to close the window, but Mr. Henshaw's voice arrested her.

"And suppose he is not there?" he said.

Mrs. Henshaw reflected. "If he is not there bring Ted Stokes back with you," she said at last, "and if he says you're George, I'll let you in."

The Changeling

The window closed and the light disappeared. Mr. Henshaw waited for some time, but in vain, and, with a very clear idea of the reception he would meet with at the hands of Mr. Stokes, set off to his lodging.

If anything, he had underestimated his friend's powers. Mr. Stokes, rudely disturbed just as he had got into bed, was the incarnation of wrath. He was violent, bitter, and insulting in a breath, but Mr. Henshaw was desperate, and Mr. Stokes, after vowing over and over again that nothing should induce him to accompany him back to his house, was at last so moved by his entreaties that he went upstairs and equipped himself for the journey.

"And, mind, after this I never want to see your face again," he said, as they walked swiftly back.

Mr. Henshaw made no reply. The events of the day had almost exhausted him, and silence was maintained until they reached the house. Much to his relief he heard somebody moving about upstairs after the first knock, and in a very short time the window was gently raised and Mrs. Henshaw looked out.

"What, you've come back?" she said, in a low, intense voice. "Well, of all the impudence! How dare you carry on like this?"

"It's me," said her husband.

The Changeling

"Yes, I see it is," was the reply.

"It's him right enough; it's your husband," said Mr. Stokes. "Alfred Bell has gone."

"How dare you stand there and tell me them falsehoods!" exclaimed Mrs. Henshaw. "I wonder the ground don't open and swallow you up. It's Mr. Bell, and if he don't go away I'll call the police."

Messrs. Henshaw and Stokes, amazed at their reception, stood blinking up at her. Then they conferred in whispers.

"If you can't tell 'em apart, how do you know this is Mr. Bell?" inquired Mr. Stokes, turning to the window again.

"How do I know?" repeated Mrs. Henshaw. "How do I know? Why, because my husband came home almost directly Mr. Bell had gone. I wonder he didn't meet him."

"Came home?" cried Mr. Henshaw, shrilly. "*Came home?*"

"Yes; and don't make so much noise," said Mrs. Henshaw, tartly; "he's asleep."

The two gentlemen turned and gazed at each other in stupefaction. Mr. Stokes was the first to recover, and, taking his dazed friend by the arm, led him gently away. At the end of the street he took a deep breath, and, after a slight pause to collect his scattered energies, summed up the situation.

The Changeling

" Mr. Stokes, taking his dazed friend by the arm, led him
gently away."

"She's twigged it all along," he said, with conviction. "You'll have to come home with me to-night, and to-morrow the best thing you can do is to make a clean breast of it. It was a silly game, and, if you remember, I was against it from the first."

MIXED RELATIONS

Mixed Relations

THE brig *Elizabeth Barstow* came up the river as though in a hurry to taste again the joys of the Metropolis. The skipper, leaning on the wheel, was in the midst of a hot discussion with the mate, who was placing before him the hygienic, economical, and moral advantages of total abstinence in language of great strength but little variety.

" Teetotallers eat more," said the skipper, finally. The mate choked, and his eye sought the galley. " Eat more? " he spluttered. " Yesterday the meat was like brick-bats; to-day it tasted like a bit o' dirty sponge. I've lived on biscuits this trip; and the only tater I ate I'm going to see a doctor about direckly I get ashore. It's a sin and a shame to spoil good food the way 'e does."

" The moment I can ship another cook he goes," said the skipper. " He seems busy, judging by the noise."

" I'm making him clean up everything, ready for

the next," explained the mate, grimly. " And he 'ad the cheek to tell me he's improving—improving ! "

" He'll go as soon as I get another," repeated the skipper, stooping and peering ahead. " I don't like being poisoned any more than you do. He told me he could cook when I shipped him; said his sister had taught him."

The mate grunted and, walking away, relieved his mind by putting his head in at the galley and bidding the cook hold up each separate utensil for his inspection. A hole in the frying-pan the cook modestly attributed to elbow-grease.

The river narrowed, and the brig, picking her way daintily through the traffic, sought her old berth at Buller's Wharf. It was occupied by a deaf sailing-barge, which, moved at last by self-interest, not unconnected with its paint, took up a less desirable position and consoled itself with adjectives.

The men on the wharf had gone for the day, and the crew of the *Elizabeth Barstow,* after making fast, went below to prepare themselves for an evening ashore. Standing before the largest saucepan-lid in the galley, the cook was putting the finishing touches to his toilet.

A light, quick step on the wharf attracted the attention of the skipper as he leaned against the side smoking. It stopped just behind him, and turning

Mixed Relations

round he found himself gazing into the soft brown eyes of the prettiest girl he had ever seen.

" Is Mr. Jewell on board, please? " she asked, with a smile.

" Jewell? " repeated the skipper. " Jewell? Don't know the name."

" He *was* on board," said the girl, somewhat taken aback. " This is the *Elizabeth Barstow*, isn't it? "

" What's his Christian name," inquired the skipper, thoughtfully.

" Albert," replied the girl. " Bert," she added, as the other shook his head.

" Oh, the cook! " said the skipper. " I didn't know his name was Jewell. Yes, he's in the galley."

He stood eyeing her and wondering in a dazed fashion what she could see in a small, white-faced, slab-sided——

The girl broke in upon his meditations. " How does he cook? " she inquired, smiling.

He was about to tell her, when he suddenly remembered the cook's statement as to his instructor. " He's getting on," he said, slowly; " he's getting on. Are you his sister? "

The girl smiled and nodded. " Ye—es," she said, slowly. " Will you tell him I am waiting for him, please? "

33

Mixed Relations

The skipper started and drew himself up; then he walked forward and put his head in at the galley.

" Bert," he said, in a friendly voice, " your sister wants to see you."

" *Who?* " inquired Mr. Jewell, in the accents of amazement. He put his head out at the door and nodded, and then, somewhat red in the face with the exercise, drew on his jacket and walked towards her. The skipper followed.

" Thank you," said the girl, with a pleasant smile.

" You're quite welcome," said the skipper.

Mr. Jewell stepped ashore and, after a moment of indecision, shook hands with his visitor.

" If you're down this way again," said the skipper, as they turned away, " perhaps you'd like to see the cabin. We're in rather a pickle just now, but if you should happen to come down for Bert to-morrow night——"

The girl's eyes grew mirthful and her lips trembled. " Thank you," she said.

" Some people like looking over cabins," murmured the skipper.

He raised his hand to his cap and turned away. The mate, who had just come on deck, stared after the retreating couple and gave vent to a low whistle.

" What a fine gal to pick up with Slushy," he remarked.

" It's his sister," said the skipper, somewhat sharply.

" The one that taught him to cook? " said the other, hastily. " Here! I'd like five minutes alone with her; I'd give 'er a piece o' my mind that 'ud do her good. I'd learn 'er. I'd tell her wot I thought of her."

" That'll do," said the skipper; " that'll do. He's not so bad for a beginner; I've known worse."

" Not so bad? " repeated the mate. " Not so bad? Why "—his voice trembled—" ain't you going to give 'im the chuck, then? "

" I shall try him for another vy'ge, George," said the skipper. " It's hard lines on a youngster if he don't have a chance. I was never one to be severe. Live and let live, that's my motto. Do as you'd be done by."

" You're turning soft-'arted in your old age," grumbled the mate.

" Old age! " said the other, in a startled voice. " Old age! I'm not thirty-seven yet."

" You're getting on," said the mate; " besides, you look old."

The skipper investigated the charge in the cabin looking-glass ten minutes later. He twisted his beard in his hand and tried to imagine how he would look without it. As a compromise he went out and had it cut short and trimmed to a point. The glass smiled approval on his return; the mate smiled too, and, being caught in the act, said it made him look like his own grandson.

It was late when the cook returned, but the skipper was on deck, and, stopping him for a match, entered into a little conversation. Mr. Jewell, surprised at first, soon became at his ease, and, the talk drifting in some unknown fashion to Miss Jewell, discussed her with brotherly frankness.

" You spent the evening together, I s'pose?" said the skipper, carelessly.

Mr. Jewell glanced at him from the corner of his eye. " Cooking," he said, and put his hand over his mouth with some suddenness.

By the time they parted the skipper had his hand in a friendly fashion on the cook's shoulder, and was displaying an interest in his welfare as unusual as it was gratifying. So unaccustomed was Mr. Jewell to such consideration that he was fain to pause for a moment or two to regain control of his features before plunging into the lamp-lit fo'c'sle.

The mate made but a poor breakfast next morning, but his superior, who saw the hand of Miss Jewell in the muddy coffee and the cremated bacon, ate his with relish. He was looking forward to the evening, the cook having assured him that his sister had ac-

Mixed Relations

" The mate smiled too."

cepted his invitation to inspect the cabin, and indeed had talked of little else. The boy was set to work house-cleaning, and, having gleaned a few particulars, cursed the sex with painstaking thoroughness.

It seemed to the skipper a favorable omen that Miss Jewell descended the companion-ladder as though to the manner born; and her exclamations of delight at the cabin completed his satisfaction. The cook, who had followed them below with some trepidation, became reassured, and seating himself on a locker joined modestly in the conversation.

" It's like a doll's-house," declared the girl, as she finished by examining the space-saving devices in the state-room. " Well, I mustn't take up any more of your time."

" I've got nothing to do," said the skipper, hastily. " I—I was thinking of going for a walk; but it's lonely walking about by yourself."

Miss Jewell agreed. She lowered her eyes and looked under the lashes at the skipper.

" I never had a sister," continued the latter, in melancholy accents.

" I don't suppose you would want to take her out if you had," said the girl.

The skipper protested. " Bert takes you out," he said.

Mixed Relations

" He isn't like most brothers," said Miss Jewell, shifting along the locker and placing her hand affectionately on the cook's shoulder.

" If I had a sister," continued the skipper, in a somewhat uneven voice, " I should take her out. This evening, for instance, I should take her to a theatre."

Miss Jewell turned upon him the innocent face of a child. " It would be nice to be your sister," she said, calmly.

The skipper attempted to speak, but his voice failed him. " Well, pretend you are my sister," he said, at last, " and we'll go to one."

" Pretend? " said Miss Jewell, as she turned and eyed the cook. " Bert wouldn't like that," she said, decidedly.

" N—no," said the cook, nervously, avoiding the skipper's eye.

" It wouldn't be proper," said Miss Jewell, sitting upright and looking very proper indeed.

" I—I meant Bert to come, too," said the skipper; " of course," he added.

The severity of Miss Jewell's expression relaxed. She stole an amused glance at the cook and, reading her instructions in his eye, began to temporize. Ten minutes later the crew of the *Elizabeth Barstow* in various attitudes of astonishment beheld their commander going ashore with his cook. The mate so far forgot himself as to whistle, but with great presence of mind cuffed the boy's ear as the skipper turned.

For some little distance the three walked along in silence. The skipper was building castles in the air, the cook was not quite at his ease, and the girl, gazing steadily in front of her, appeared slightly embarrassed.

By the time they reached Aldgate and stood waiting for an omnibus Miss Jewell found herself assailed by doubts. She remembered that she did not want to go to a theatre, and warmly pressed the two men to go together and leave her to go home. The skipper remonstrated in vain, but the cook came to the rescue, and Miss Jewell, still protesting, was pushed on to a 'bus and propelled upstairs. She took a vacant seat in front, and the skipper and Mr. Jewell shared one behind.

The three hours at the theatre passed all too soon, although the girl was so interested in the performance that she paid but slight attention to her companions. During the waits she became interested in her surroundings, and several times called the skipper's attention to smart-looking men in the stalls and boxes. At one man she stared so persistently that an opera-glass was at last levelled in return.

"How rude of him," she said, smiling sweetly at the skipper.

She shook her head in disapproval, but the next moment he saw her gazing steadily at the opera-glasses again.

"If you don't look he'll soon get tired of it," he said, between his teeth.

"Yes, perhaps he will," said Miss Jewell, without lowering her eyes in the least.

The skipper sat in torment until the lights were lowered and the curtain went up again. When it fell he began to discuss the play, but Miss Jewell returned such vague replies that it was evident her thoughts were far away.

"I wonder who he is?" she whispered, gazing meditatingly at the box.

"A waiter, I should think," snapped the skipper.

The girl shook her head. "No, he is much too distinguished-looking," she said, seriously. "Well, I suppose he'll know me again."

The skipper felt that he wanted to get up and smash things; beginning with the man in the box. It was his first love episode for nearly ten years, and he had forgotten the pains and penalties which attach to the condition. When the performance was over he darted a threatening glance at the box, and, keeping close to Miss Jewell, looked carefully about him to make sure that they were not followed.

" It was ripping," said the cook, as they emerged into the fresh air.

" Lovely," said the girl, in a voice of gentle melancholy. " I shall come and see it again, perhaps, when you are at sea."

" Not alone? " said the skipper, in a startled voice.

" I don't mind being alone," said Miss Jewell, gently; " I'm used to it."

The other's reply was lost in the rush for the 'bus, and for the second time that evening the skipper had to find fault with the seating arrangements. And when a vacancy by the side of Miss Jewell did occur, he was promptly forestalled by a young man in a check suit smoking a large cigar.

They got off at Aldgate, and the girl thanked him for a pleasant evening. A hesitating offer to see her home was at once negatived, and the skipper, watching her and the cook until they disappeared in the traffic, walked slowly and thoughtfully to his ship.

The brig sailed the next evening at eight o'clock, and it was not until six that the cook remarked, in the most casual manner, that his sister was coming down to see him off. She arrived half an hour late, and, so far from wanting to see the cabin again, discovered an inconvenient love of fresh air. She came down at last, at the instance of the cook, and, once below, her mood changed, and she treated the skipper with a soft graciousness which raised him to the seventh heaven. "You'll be good to Bert, won't you?" she inquired, with a smile at that young man.

"I'll treat him like my own brother," said the skipper, fervently. "No, better than that; I'll treat him like your brother."

The cook sat erect and, the skipper being occupied with Miss Jewell, winked solemnly at the sky-light.

"I know *you* will," said the girl, very softly; "but I don't think the men——"

"The men'll do as I wish," said the skipper, sternly. "I'm the master on this ship—she's half mine, too—and anybody who interferes with him interferes with me. If there's anything you don't like, Bert, you tell me."

Mr. Jewell, his small, black eyes sparkling, promised, and then, muttering something about his work, exchanged glances with the girl and went up on deck.

"It is a nice cabin," said Miss Jewell, shifting an inch and a half nearer to the skipper. "I suppose poor Bert has to have his meals in that stuffy little place at the other end of the ship, doesn't he?"

"The fo'c'sle?" said the skipper, struggling between love and discipline. "Yes."

Mixed Relations

The girl sighed, and the mate, who was listening at the skylight above, held his breath with anxiety. Miss Jewell sighed again and in an absent-minded fashion increased the distance between herself and companion by six inches.

" It's usual," faltered the skipper.

" Yes, of course," said the girl, coldly.

" But if Bert likes to feed here, he's welcome," said the skipper, desperately, " and he can sleep aft, too. The mate can say what he likes."

The mate rose and, walking forward, raised his clenched fists to heaven and availed himself of the permission to the fullest extent of a somewhat extensive vocabulary.

" Do you know what I think you are? " inquired Miss Jewell, bending towards him with a radiant face.

" No," said the other, trembling. " What? "

The girl paused. " It wouldn't do to tell you," she said, in a low voice. " It might make you vain."

" Do you know what I think you are? " inquired the skipper in his turn.

Miss Jewell eyed him composedly, albeit the corners of her mouth trembled. " Yes," she said, unexpectedly.

Steps sounded above and came heavily down the

companion-ladder. " Tide's a'most on the turn,"
said the mate, gruffly, from the door.

The skipper hesitated, but the mate stood aside for
the girl to pass, and he followed her up on deck
and assisted her to the jetty. For hours afterwards
he debated with himself whether she really had allowed her hand to stay in his a second or two longer
than necessary, or whether unconscious muscular action on his part was responsible for the phenomenon.

He became despondent as they left London behind, but the necessity of interfering between a gog-
gle-eyed and obtuse mate and a pallid but no less ob-
stinate cook helped to relieve him.

" He says he is going to sleep aft," choked the
mate, pointing to the cook's bedding.

" Quite right," said the skipper. " I told him to.
He's going to take his meals here, too. Anything to
say against it? "

The mate sat down on a locker and fought for
breath. The cook, still pale, felt his small, black
mustache and eyed him with triumphant malice. " I
told 'im they was your orders," he remarked.

" And I told him I didn't believe him," said the
mate. " Nobody would. Whoever 'eard of a cook
living aft? Why, they'd laugh at the idea."

He laughed himself, but in a strangely mirthless
fashion, and, afraid to trust himself, went up on deck

and brooded savagely apart. Nor did he come down to breakfast until the skipper and cook had finished.

Mr. Jewell bore his new honors badly, and the inability to express their dissatisfaction by means of violence had a bad effect on the tempers of the crew. Sarcasm they did try, but at that the cook could more than hold his own, and, although the men doubted his ability at first, he was able to prove to them by actual experiment that he could cook worse than they supposed.

The brig reached her destination—Creekhaven— on the fifth day, and Mr. Jewell found himself an honored guest at the skipper's cottage. It was a comfortable place, but, as the cook pointed out, too large for one. He also referred, incidentally, to his sister's love of a country life, and, finding himself on a subject of which the other never tired, gave full reins to a somewhat picturesque imagination.

They were back at London within the fortnight, and the skipper learned to his dismay that Miss Jewell was absent on a visit. In these circumstances he would have clung to the cook, but that gentleman, pleading engagements, managed to elude him for two nights out of the three.

On the third day Miss Jewell returned to London, and, making her way to the wharf, was just in time to wave farewells as the brig parted from the wharf.

Mixed Relations

"Sarcasm they did try, but at that the cook could more than hold his own."

Mixed Relations

From the fact that the cook was not visible at the moment the skipper took the salutation to himself. It cheered him for the time, but the next day he was so despondent that the cook, by this time thoroughly in his confidence, offered to write when they got to Creekhaven and fix up an evening.

" And there's really no need for you to come, Bert," said the skipper, cheering up.

Mr. Jewell shook his head. " She wouldn't go without me," he said, gravely. " You've no idea 'ow particular she is. Always was from a child."

" Well, we might lose you," said the skipper, reflecting. " How would that be? "

" We might try it," said the cook, without enthusiasm.

To his dismay the skipper, before they reached London again, had invented at least a score of ways by which he might enjoy Miss Jewell's company without the presence of a third person, some of them so ingenious that the cook, despite his utmost efforts, could see no way of opposing them.

The skipper put his ideas into practice as soon as they reached London. Between Wapping and Charing Cross he lost the cook three times. Miss Jewell found him twice, and the third time she was so difficult that the skipper had to join in the treasure-hunt himself. The cook listened unmoved to a highly-colored picture of his carelessness from the lips of Miss Jewell, and bestowed a sympathetic glance upon the skipper as she paused for breath.

"It's as bad as taking a child out," said the latter, with well-affected indignation.

"Worse," said the girl, tightening her lips.

With a perseverance worthy of a better cause the skipper nudged the cook's arm and tried again. This time he was successful beyond his wildest dreams, and, after ten minutes' frantic search, found that he had lost them both. He wandered up and down for hours, and it was past eleven when he returned to the ship and found the cook waiting for him.

"We thought something 'ad happened to you," said the cook. "Kate has been in a fine way about it. Five minutes after you lost me she found me, and we've been hunting 'igh and low ever since."

Miss Jewell expressed her relief the next evening, and, stealing a glance at the face of the skipper, experienced a twinge of something which she took to be remorse. Ignoring the cook's hints as to theatres, she elected to go for a long 'bus ride, and, sitting in front with the skipper, left Mr. Jewell to keep a chaperon's eye on them from three seats behind.

Conversation was for some time disjointed; then the brightness and crowded state of the streets led

the skipper to sound his companion as to her avowed
taste for a country life.

" I should love it," said Miss Jewell, with a sigh.
" But there's no chance of it; I've got my living to
earn."

" You might—might marry somebody living in
the country," said the skipper, in trembling tones.

Miss Jewell shuddered. " Marry!" she said,
scornfully.

" Most people do," said the other.

" Sensible people don't," said the girl. " You
haven't," she added, with a smile.

" I'm very thankful I haven't," retorted the skipper, with great meaning.

" There you are!" said the girl, triumphantly.

" I never saw anybody I liked," said the skipper,
" be—before."

" If ever I did marry," said Miss Jewell, with
remarkable composure, " if ever I was foolish
enough to do such a thing, I think I would marry a
man a few years younger than myself."

" Younger?" said the dismayed skipper.

Miss Jewell nodded. " They make the best hus-
bands," she said, gravely.

The skipper began to argue the point, and Mr.
Jewell, at that moment taking a seat behind, joined
in with some heat. A more ardent supporter could

not have been found, although his repetition of the phrase " May and December " revealed a want of tact of which the skipper had not thought him capable. What had promised to be a red-letter day in his existence was spoiled, and he went to bed that night with the full conviction that he had better abandon a project so hopeless.

With a fine morning his courage revived, but as voyage succeeded voyage he became more and more perplexed. The devotion of the cook was patent to all men, but Miss Jewell was as changeable as a weather-glass. The skipper would leave her one night convinced that he had better forget her as soon as possible, and the next her manner would be so kind, and her glances so soft, that only the presence of the ever-watchful cook prevented him from proposing on the spot. The end came one evening in October. The skipper had hurried back from the City, laden with stores, Miss Jewell having, after many refusals, consented to grace the tea-table that afternoon. The table, set by the boy, groaned beneath the weight of unusual luxuries, but the girl had not arrived. The cook was also missing, and the only occupant of the cabin was the mate, who, sitting at one corner, was eating with great relish.

" Ain't you going to get your tea? " he inquired.

" No hurry," said the skipper, somewhat incensed

at his haste. " It wouldn't have hurt *you* to have waited a bit."

" Waited? " said the other. " What for? "

" For my visitors," was the reply.

The mate bit a piece off a crust and stirred his tea. " No use waiting for them," he said, with a grin. " They ain't coming."

" What do you mean? " demanded the skipper.

" I mean," said the mate, continuing to stir his tea with great enjoyment—" I mean that all that kind'artedness of yours was clean chucked away on that cook. He's got a berth ashore and he's gone for good. He left you 'is love; he left it with Bill Hemp."

" Berth ashore? " said the skipper, staring.

" Ah! " said the mate, taking a large and noisy sip from his cup. " He's been fooling you all along for what he could get out of you. Sleeping aft and feeding aft, nobody to speak a word to 'im, and going out and being treated by the skipper; Bill said he laughed so much when he was telling 'im that the tears was running down 'is face like rain. He said he'd never been treated so much in his life."

" That'll do," said the skipper, quickly.

" You ought to hear Bill tell it," said the mate, regretfully. " I can't do it anything like as well as what he can. Made us all roar, he did. What amused 'em most was you thinking that that gal was cookie's sister."

The skipper, with a sharp exclamation, leaned forward, staring at him.

" They're going to be married at Christmas," said the mate, choking in his cup.

The skipper sat upright again, and tried manfully to compose his features. Many things he had not understood before were suddenly made clear, and he remembered now the odd way in which the girl had regarded him as she bade him good-night on the previous evening. The mate eyed him with interest, and was about to supply him with further details when his attention was attracted by footsteps descending the companion-ladder. Then he put down his cup with great care, and stared in stolid amazement at the figure of Miss Jewell in the doorway.

" I'm a bit late," she said, flushing slightly.

She crossed over and shook hands with the skipper, and, in the most natural fashion in the world, took a seat and began to remove her gloves. The mate swung round and regarded her open-mouthed; the skipper, whose ideas were in a whirl, sat regarding her in silence. The mate was the first to move; he left the cabin rubbing his shin, and casting furious glances at the skipper.

Mixed Relations

"You didn't expect to see me?" said the girl, reddening again.

"No," was the reply.

The girl looked at the tablecloth. "I came to beg your pardon," she said, in a low voice.

"There's nothing to beg my pardon for," said the skipper, clearing his throat. "By rights I ought to beg yours. You did quite right to make fun of me. I can see it now."

"When you asked me whether I was Bert's sister I didn't like to say 'no,' continued the girl; "and at first I let you come out with me for the fun of the thing, and then Bert said it would be good for him, and then—then——"

"Yes," said the skipper, after a long pause.

The girl broke a biscuit into small pieces, and arranged them on the cloth. "Then I didn't mind your coming so much," she said, in a low voice.

The skipper caught his breath and tried to gaze at the averted face.

The girl swept the crumbs aside and met his gaze squarely. "Not quite so much," she explained.

"I've been a fool," said the skipper. "I've been a fool. I've made myself a laughing-stock all round, but if I could have it all over again I would."

"That can never be," said the girl, shaking her head. "Bert wouldn't come."

Mixed Relations

"'Good-by,' he said, slowly; 'and I wish you both every happiness.'"

"No, of course not," asserted the other.

The girl bit her lip. The skipper thought that he had never seen her eyes so large and shining. There was a long silence.

"Good-by," said the girl at last, rising.

The skipper rose to follow. "Good-by," he said, slowly; "and I wish you both every happiness."

"Happiness?" echoed the girl, in a surprised voice. "Why?"

"When you are married."

"I am not going to be married," said the girl. "I told Bert so this afternoon. Good-by."

The skipper actually let her get nearly to the top of the ladder before he regained his presence of mind. Then, in obedience to a powerful tug at the hem of her skirt, she came down again, and accompanied him meekly back to the cabin.

HIS LORDSHIP

His Lordship

FARMER ROSE sat in his porch smoking an evening pipe. By his side, in a comfortable Windsor chair, sat his friend the miller, also smoking, and gazing with half-closed eyes at the landscape as he listened for the thousandth time to his host's complaints about his daughter.

"The long and the short of it is, Cray," said the farmer, with an air of mournful pride, "she's far too good-looking."

Mr. Cray grunted.

"Truth is truth, though she's my daughter," continued Mr. Rose, vaguely. "She's too good-looking. Sometimes when I've taken her up to market I've seen the folks fair turn their backs on the cattle and stare at her instead."

Mr. Cray sniffed; louder, perhaps, than he had intended. "Beautiful that rose-bush smells," he remarked, as his friend turned and eyed him.

"What is the consequence?" demanded the farmer, relaxing his gaze. "She looks in the glass and sees herself, and then she gets miserable and uppish because there ain't nobody in these parts good enough for her to marry."

" It's a extraordinary thing to me where she gets them good looks from," said the miller, deliberately.

" Ah! " said Mr. Rose, and sat trying to think of a means of enlightening his friend without undue loss of modesty.

" She ain't a bit like her poor mother," mused Mr. Cray.

" No, she don't get her looks from her," assented the other.

" It's one o' them things you can't account for," said Mr. Cray, who was very tired of the subject; " it's just like seeing a beautiful flower blooming on an old cabbage-stump."

The farmer knocked his pipe out noisily and began to refill it. "People have said that she takes after me a trifle," he remarked, shortly.

" You weren't fool enough to believe that, I know," said the miller. " Why, she's no more like you than you're like a warming-pan — not so much."

Mr. Rose regarded his friend fixedly. " You ain't got a very nice way o' putting things, Cray," he said, mournfully.

" I'm no flatterer," said the miller; " never was.

His Lordship

And you can't please everybody. If I said your daughter took after you I don't s'pose she'd ever speak to me again."

"The worst of it is," said the farmer, disregarding his remark, "she won't settle down. There's young Walter Lomas after her now, and she won't look at him. He's a decent young fellow is Walter, and she's been and named one o' the pigs after him, and the way she mixes them up together is disgraceful."

"If she was my girl she should marry young Walter," said the miller, firmly. "What's wrong with him?"

"She looks higher," replied the other, mysteriously; "she's always reading them romantic books full o' love tales, and she's never tired o' talking of a girl her mother used to know that went on the stage and married a baronet. She goes and sits in the best parlor every afternoon now, and calls it the drawing-room. She'll sit there till she's past the marrying age, and then she'll turn round and blame me."

"She wants a lesson," said Mr. Cray, firmly. "She wants to be taught her position in life, not to go about turning up her nose at young men and naming pigs after them."

Mr. Rose sighed.

"What she wants to understand is that the upper classes wouldn't look at her," pursued the miller.

His Lordship

" It would be easier to make her understand that if they didn't," said the farmer.

" I mean," said Mr. Cray, sternly, " with a view to marriage. What you ought to do is to get somebody staying down here with you pretending to be a lord or a nobleman, and ordering her about and not noticing her good looks at all. Then, while she's upset about that, in comes Walter Lomas to comfort her and be a contrast to the other."

Mr. Rose withdrew his pipe and regarded him open-mouthed.

" Yes; but how——" he began.

" And it seems to me," interrupted Mr. Cray, " that I know just the young fellow to do it—nephew of my wife's. He was coming to stay a fortnight with us, but you can have him with pleasure—me and him don't get on over and above well."

" Perhaps he wouldn't do it," objected the farmer.

" He'd do it like a shot," said Mr. Cray, positively. " It would be fun for us and it 'ud be a lesson for her. If you like, I'll tell him to write to you for lodgings, as he wants to come for a fortnight's fresh air after the fatiguing gayeties of town."

" Fatiguing gayeties of town," repeated the admiring farmer. " Fatiguing——"

He sat back in his chair and laughed, and Mr. Cray, delighted at the prospect of getting rid so easily of a tiresome guest, laughed too. Overhead at the open window a third person laughed, but in so quiet and well-bred a fashion that neither of them heard her.

The farmer received a letter a day or two afterwards, and negotiations between Jane Rose on the one side and Lord Fairmount on the other were soon in progress; the farmer's own composition being deemed somewhat crude for such a correspondence.

" I wish he didn't want it kept so secret," said Miss Rose, pondering over the final letter. " I should like to let the Crays and one or two more people know he is staying with us. However, I suppose he must have his own way."

" You must do as he wishes," said her father, using his handkerchief violently.

Jane sighed. " He'll be a little company for me, at any rate," she remarked. " What is the matter, father?"

" Bit of a cold," said the farmer, indistinctly, as he made for the door, still holding his handkerchief to his face. " Been coming on some time."

He put on his hat and went out, and Miss Rose, watching him from the window, was not without fears that the joke might prove too much for a man of his habit. She regarded him thoughtfully, and when he returned at one o'clock to dinner, and encountered instead a violent dust-storm which was raging in the house, she noted with pleasure that his sense of humor was more under control.

" Dinner? " she said, as he strove to squeeze past the furniture which was piled in the hall. " We've got no time to think of dinner, and if we had there's no place for you to eat it. You'd better go in the larder and cut yourself a crust of bread and cheese."

Her father hesitated and glared at the servant, who, with her head bound up in a duster, passed at the double with a broom. Then he walked slowly into the kitchen.

Miss Rose called out something after him.

" Eh? " said her father, coming back hopefully.

" How is your cold, dear? "

The farmer made no reply, and his daughter smiled contentedly as she heard him stamping about in the larder. He made but a poor meal, and then, refusing point-blank to assist Annie in moving the piano, went and smoked a very reflective pipe in the garden.

Lord Fairmount arrived the following day on foot from the station, and after acknowledging the farmer's salute with a distant nod requested him to send a cart for his luggage. He was a tall, good-looking young man, and as he stood in the hall languidly

His Lordship

" ' She's got your eyes,' said his lordship."

twisting his mustache Miss Rose deliberately decided upon his destruction.

" These your daughters? " he inquired, carelessly, as he followed his host into the parlor.

" One of 'em is, my lord; the other is my servant," replied the farmer.

" She's got your eyes," said his lordship, tapping the astonished Annie under the chin; " your nose too, I think."

" That's my servant," said the farmer, knitting his brows at him.

" Oh, indeed! " said his lordship, airily.

He turned round and regarded Jane, but, although she tried to meet him half-way by elevating her chin a little, his audacity failed him and the words died away on his tongue. A long silence followed, broken only by the ill-suppressed giggles of Annie, who had retired to the kitchen.

" I trust that we shall make your lordship comfortable," said Miss Rose.

" I hope so, my good girl," was the reply. " And now will you show me my room? "

Miss Rose led the way upstairs and threw open the door; Lord Fairmount, pausing on the threshold, gazed at it disparagingly.

" Is this the best room you have? " he inquired, stiffly.

His Lordship

" Oh, no," said Miss Rose, smiling; " father's room is much better than this. Look here."

She threw open another door and, ignoring a gesticulating figure which stood in the hall below, regarded him anxiously. " If you would prefer father's room he would be delighted for you to have it. Delighted."

" Yes, I will have this one," said Lord Fairmount, entering. " Bring me up some hot water, please, and clear these boots and leggings out."

Miss Rose tripped downstairs and, bestowing a witching smile upon her sire, waved away his request for an explanation and hastened into the kitchen, whence Annie shortly afterwards emerged with the water.

It was with something of a shock that the farmer discovered that he had to wait for his dinner while his lordship had luncheon. That meal, under his daughter's management, took a long time, and the joint when it reached him was more than half cold. It was, moreover, quite clear that the aristocracy had not even mastered the rudiments of carving, but preferred instead to box the compass for tit-bits.

He ate his meal in silence, and when it was over sought out his guest to administer a few much-needed stage-directions. Owing, however, to the ubiquity of Jane he wasted nearly the whole of the afternoon

67

His Lordship

before he obtained an opportunity. Even then the interview was short, the farmer having to compress into ten seconds instructions for Lord Fairmount to express a desire to take his meals with the family, and his dinner at the respectable hour of 1 p.m. Instructions as to a change of bedroom were frustrated by the reappearance of Jane.

His lordship went for a walk after that, and coming back with a bored air stood on the hearth-rug in the living-room and watched Miss Rose sewing.

" Very dull place," he said at last, in a dissatis-fied voice.

" Yes, my lord," said Miss Rose, demurely.

" Fearfully dull," complained his lordship, stifling a yawn. " What I'm to do to amuse myself for a fortnight I'm sure I don't know."

Miss Rose raised her fine eyes and regarded him intently. Many a lesser man would have looked no farther for amusement.

" I'm afraid there is not much to do about here, my lord," she said quietly. " We are very plain folk in these parts."

" Yes," assented the other. An obvious compli-ment rose of itself to his lips, but he restrained him-self, though with difficulty. Miss Rose bent her head over her work and stitched industriously. His lord-

His Lordship

ship took up a book and, remembering his mission, read for a couple of hours without taking the slightest notice of her. Miss Rose glanced over in his direction once or twice, and then, with a somewhat vixenish expression on her delicate features, resumed her sewing.

"Wonderful eyes she's got," said the gentleman, as he sat on the edge of his bed that night and thought over the events of the day. "It's pretty to see them flash."

He saw them flash several times during the next few days, and Mr. Rose himself, was more than satisfied with the hauteur with which his guest treated the household.

"But I don't like the way you have with me," he complained.

"It's all in the part," urged his lordship.

"Well, you can leave that part out," rejoined Mr. Rose, with some acerbity. "I object to being spoke to as you speak to me before that girl Annie. Be as proud and unpleasant as you like to my daughter, but leave me alone. Mind that!"

His lordship promised, and in pursuance of his host's instructions strove manfully to subdue feelings towards Miss Rose by no means in accordance with them. The best of us are liable to absent-mindedness, and he sometimes so far forgot himself as to address her in tones as humble as any in her somewhat large experience.

" I hope that we are making you comfortable here, my lord? " she said, as they sat together one afternoon.

" I have never been more comfortable in my life," was the gracious reply.

Miss Rose shook her head. " Oh, my lord," she said, in protest, " think of your mansion."

His lordship thought of it. For two or three days he had been thinking of houses and furniture and other things of that nature.

" I have never seen an old country seat," continued Miss Rose, clasping her hands and gazing at him wistfully. " I should be so grateful if your lordship would describe yours to me."

His lordship shifted uneasily, and then, in face of the girl's persistence, stood for some time divided between the contending claims of Hampton Court Palace and the Tower of London. He finally decided upon the former, after first refurnishing it at Maple's.

" How happy you must be! " said the breathless Jane, when he had finished.

He shook his head gravely. " My possessions have never given me any happiness," he remarked. " I would much rather be in a humble rank of life. Live where I like, and—and marry whom I like."

There was no mistaking the meaning fall in his voice. Miss Rose sighed gently and lowered her eyes—her lashes had often excited comment. Then, in a soft voice, she asked him the sort of life he would prefer.

In reply, his lordship, with an eloquence which surprised himself, portrayed the joys of life in a seven-roomed house in town, with a greenhouse six feet by three, and a garden large enough to contain it. He really spoke well, and when he had finished his listener gazed at him with eyes suffused with timid admiration.

"Oh, my lord," she said, prettily, "now I know what you've been doing. You've been slumming."

"Slumming?" gasped his lordship.

"You couldn't have described a place like that unless you had been," said Miss Rose nodding. "I hope you took the poor people some nice hot soup."

His lordship tried to explain, but without success. Miss Rose persisted in regarding him as a missionary of food and warmth, and spoke feelingly of the people who had to live in such places. She also warned him against the risk of infection.

"You don't understand," he repeated, impatiently. "These are nice houses—nice enough for anybody to live in. If you took soup to people like that, why, they'd throw it at you."

" Wretches ! " murmured the indignant Jane, who was enjoying herself amazingly.

His lordship eyed her with sudden suspicion, but her face was quite grave and bore traces of strong feeling. He explained again, but without avail.

" You never ought to go near such places, my lord," she concluded, solemnly, as she rose to quit the room. " Even a girl of my station would draw the line at that."

She bowed deeply and withdrew. His lordship sank into a chair and, thrusting his hands into his pockets, gazed gloomily at the dried grasses in the grate.

During the next day or two his appetite failed, and other well-known symptoms set in. Miss Rose, diagnosing them all, prescribed by stealth some bitter remedies. The farmer regarded his change of manner with disapproval, and, concluding that it was due to his own complaints, sought to reassure him. He also pointed out that his daughter's opinion of the aristocracy was hardly likely to increase if the only member she knew went about the house as though he had just lost his grandmother.

" You are longing for the gayeties of town, my lord," he remarked one morning at breakfast.

His Lordship

His lordship shook his head. The gayeties comprised, amongst other things, a stool and a desk.

" I don't like town," he said, with a glance at Jane. " If I had my choice I would live here always. " I would sooner live here in this charming spot with this charming society than anywhere."

Mr. Rose coughed and, having caught his eye, shook his head at him and glanced significantly over at the unconscious Jane. The young man ignored his action and, having got an opening, gave utterance in the course of the next ten minutes to Radical heresies of so violent a type that the farmer could hardly keep his seat. Social distinctions were condemned utterly, and the House of Lords referred to as a human dust-bin. The farmer gazed open-mouthed at this snake he had nourished.

" Your lordship will alter your mind when you get to town," said Jane, demurely.

" Never! " declared the other, impressively.

The girl sighed, and gazing first with much interest at her parent, who seemed to be doing his best to ward off a fit, turned her lustrous eyes upon the guest.

" We shall all miss you," she said, softly. " You've been a lesson to all of us."

" Lesson? " he repeated, flushing.

His Lordship

" It has improved our behavior so, having a lord in the house," said Miss Rose, with painful humility. " I'm sure father hasn't been like the same man since you've been here."

" What d'ye mean Miss? " demanded the farmer, hotly.

" Don't speak like that before his lordship, father," said his daughter, hastily. " I'm not blaming you; you're no worse than the other men about here. You haven't had an opportunity of learning before, that's all. It isn't your fault."

" Learning? " bellowed the farmer, turning an inflamed visage upon his apprehensive guest. " Have you noticed anything wrong about my behavior? "

" Certainly not," said his lordship, hastily.

" All I know is," continued Miss Rose, positively, " I wish you were going to stay here another six months for father's sake."

" Look here——" began Mr. Rose, smiting the table.

" And Annie's," said Jane, raising her voice above the din. " I don't know which has improved the most. I'm sure the way they both drink their tea now——"

Mr. Rose pushed his chair back loudly and got up from the table. For a moment he stood struggling

74

for words, then he turned suddenly with a growl and quitted the room, banging the door after him in a fashion which clearly indicated that he still had some lessons to learn.

" You've made your father angry," said his lord-ship.

" It's for his own good," said Miss Rose. " Are you really sorry to leave us? "

" Sorry? " repeated the other. " Sorry is no word for it."

" You will miss father," said the girl.

He sighed gently.

" And Annie," she continued.

He sighed again, and Jane took a slight glance at him cornerwise.

" And me too, I hope," she said, in a low voice.

" *Miss* you! " repeated his lordship, in a suffocat-ing voice. " I should miss the sun less."

" I am so glad," said Jane, clasping her hands; " it is so nice to feel that one is not quite forgotten. Of course, I can never forget you. You are the only nobleman I have ever met."

" I hope that it is not only because of that," he said, forlornly.

Miss Rose pondered. When she pondered her eyes increased in size and revealed unsuspected depths.

" No-o," she said at length, in a hesitating voice.

" Suppose that I were not what I am represented to be," he said slowly. " Suppose that, instead of being Lord Fairmount, I were merely a clerk."

" A clerk? " repeated Miss Rose, with a very well-managed shudder. " How can I suppose such an absurd thing as that? "

" But if I were? " urged his lordship, feverishly.

" It's no use supposing such a thing as that," said Miss Rose, briskly; " your high birth is stamped on you."

His lordship shook his head.

" I would sooner be a laborer on this farm than a king anywhere else," he said, with feeling.

Miss Rose drew a pattern on the floor with the toe of her shoe.

" The poorest laborer on the farm can have the pleasure of looking at you every day," continued his lordship passionately. " Every day of his life he can see you, and feel a better man for it."

Miss Rose looked at him sharply. Only the day before the poorest laborer had seen her—when he wasn't expecting the honor—and received an epitome of his character which had nearly stunned him. But his lordship's face was quite grave.

" I go to-morrow," he said.

His Lordship

" Yes," said Jane, in a hushed voice.

He crossed the room gently and took a seat by her side. Miss Rose, still gazing at the floor, wondered indignantly why it was she was not blushing. His Lordship's conversation had come to a sudden stop and the silence was most awkward.

" I've been a fool, Miss Rose," he said at last, rising and standing over her; " and I've been taking a great liberty. I've been deceiving you for nearly a fortnight."

" Nonsense! " responded Miss Rose, briskly.

" I have been deceiving you," he repeated. " I have made you believe that I am a person of title."

" Nonsense! " said Miss Rose again.

The other started and eyed her uneasily.

" Nobody would mistake you for a lord," said Miss Rose, cruelly. " Why, I shouldn't think that you had ever seen one. You didn't do it at all properly. Why, your uncle Cray would have done it better."

Mr. Cray's nephew fell back in consternation and eyed her dumbly as she laughed. All mirth is not contagious, and he was easily able to refrain from joining in this.

" I can't understand," said Miss Rose, as she wiped a tear-dimmed eye— " I can't understand how you could have thought I should be so stupid."

His Lordship

"I've been a fool," said the other, bitterly, as he retreated to the door. "Good-by."

"Good-by," said Jane. She looked him full in the face, and the blushes for which she had been waiting came in force. "You needn't go, unless you want to," she said, softly. "I like fools better than lords."

His Lordship

" 'I like fools better than lords.' "

ALF'S DREAM

Alf's Dream

I'VE just been drinking a man's health," said the
night watchman, coming slowly on to the wharf
and wiping his mouth with the back of his hand;
" he's come in for a matter of three 'undred and
twenty pounds, and he stood me arf a pint—arf a
pint ! "

He dragged a small empty towards him, and after
planing the surface with his hand sat down and gazed
scornfully across the river.

" Four ale," he said, with a hard laugh; " and
when I asked 'im—just for the look of the thing,
and to give 'im a hint—whether he'd 'ave another,
he said ' yes.' "

The night watchman rose and paced restlessly up
and down the jetty.

" Money," he said, at last, resuming his wonted
calm and lowering himself carefully to the box again
—money always gets left to the wrong people;
some of the kindest-'arted men I've ever known

83

Alf's Dream

'ave never had a ha'penny left 'em, while teetotaler arter teetotaler wot I've heard of 'ave come in for fortins."

It's 'ard lines though, sometimes, waiting for other people's money. I knew o' one chap that waited over forty years for 'is grandmother to die and leave 'im her money; and she died of catching cold at 'is funeral. Another chap I knew, arter waiting years and years for 'is rich aunt to die, was hung because she committed suicide.

It's always risky work waiting for other people to die and leave you money. Sometimes they don't die; sometimes they marry agin; and sometimes they leave it to other people instead.

Talking of marrying agin reminds me o' something that 'appened to a young fellow I knew named Alf Simms. Being an orphan 'e was brought up by his uncle, George Hatchard, a widowed man of about sixty. Alf used to go to sea off and on, but more off than on, his uncle 'aving quite a tidy bit of 'ouse property, and it being understood that Alf was to have it arter he 'ad gone. His uncle used to like to 'ave him at 'ome, and Alf didn't like work, so it suited both parties.

I used to give Alf a bit of advice sometimes, sixty being a dangerous age for a man, especially when he 'as been a widower for so long he 'as had time

to forget wot being married's like; but I must do Alf
the credit to say it wasn't wanted. He 'ad got a very
old 'ead on his shoulders, and always picked the
housekeeper 'imself to save the old man the trouble.
I saw two of 'em, and I dare say I could 'ave seen
more, only I didn't want to.

Cleverness is a good thing in its way, but there's
such a thing as being too clever, and the last 'ousekeeper young Alf picked died of old age a week arter
he 'ad gone to sea. She passed away while she was
drawing George Hatchard's supper beer, and he lost
ten gallons o' the best bitter ale and his 'ousekeeper
at the same time.

It was four months arter that afore Alf came 'ome,
and the fust sight of the new 'ousekeeper, wot opened
the door to 'im, upset 'im terrible. She was the right
side o' sixty to begin with, and only ordinary plain.
Then she was as clean as a new pin, and dressed up
as though she was going out to tea.

" Oh, you're Alfred, I s'pose? " she ses, looking
at 'im.

" Mr. Simms is my name," ses young Alf, starting
and drawing hisself up.

" I know you by your portrait," ses the 'ousekeeper. " Come in. 'Ave you 'ad a pleasant v'y'ge?
Wipe your boots."

Alfred wiped 'is boots afore he thought of wot he

was doing. Then he drew hisself up stiff agin and marched into the parlor.

" Sit down," ses the 'ousekeeper, in a kind voice.

Alfred sat down afore he thought wot 'e was doing agin.

" I always like to see people comfortable," ses the 'ousekeeper; " it's my way. It's warm weather for the time o' year, ain't it? George is upstairs, but he'll be down in a minute."

" *Who?* " ses Alf, hardly able to believe his ears.

" George," ses the 'ousekeeper.

" George? George who? " ses Alfred, very severe.

" Why your uncle, of course," ses the 'ousekeeper. " Do you think I've got a houseful of Georges? "

Young Alf sat staring at her and couldn't say a word. He noticed that the room 'ad been altered, and that there was a big photygraph of her stuck up on the mantelpiece. He sat there fidgeting with 'is feet—until the 'ousekeeper looked at them—and then 'e got up and walked upstairs.

His uncle, wot was sitting on his bed when 'e went into the room and pretended that he 'adn't heard 'im come in, shook hands with 'im as though he'd never leave off.

" I've got something to tell you, Alf," he ses, arter they 'ad said " How d'ye do? " and he 'ad talked about the weather until Alf was fair tired of it.

Alf's Dream

" I've been and gone and done a foolish thing, and
'ow you'll take it I don't know."

" Been and asked the new 'ousekeeper to marry
you, I s'pose? " ses Alf, looking at 'im very hard.

His uncle shook his 'ead. " I never asked 'er;
I'd take my Davy I didn't," he ses.

" Well, you ain't going to marry her, then? " ses
Alf, brightening up.

His uncle shook his 'ead agin. " She didn't want
no asking," he ses, speaking very slow and mournful.
" I just 'appened to put my arm round her waist by
accident one day and the thing was done."

" Accident? How could you do it by accident? "
ses Alf, firing up.

" How can I tell you that? " ses George Hatchard. " If I'd known 'ow, it wouldn't 'ave been
an accident, would it? "

" Don't you want to marry her? " ses Alf, at last.
" You needn't marry 'er if you don't want to."

George Hatchard looked at 'im and sniffed.
" When you know her as well as I do you won't talk
so foolish," he ses. " We'd better go down now, else
she'll think we've been talking about 'er."

They went downstairs and 'ad tea together, and
young Alf soon see the truth of his uncle's remarks.
Mrs. Pearce—that was the 'ousekeeper's name—
called his uncle " dear " every time she spoke to 'im,

Alf's Dream

and arter tea she sat on the sofa side by side with 'im and held his 'and.

Alf lay awake arf that night thinking things over and 'ow to get Mrs. Pearce out of the house, and he woke up next morning with it still on 'is mind. Every time he got 'is uncle alone he spoke to 'im about it, and told 'im to pack Mrs. Pearce off with a month's wages, but George Hatchard wouldn't listen to 'im.

" She'd 'ave me up for breach of promise and ruin me," he ses. " She reads the paper to me every Sunday arternoon, mostly breach of promise cases, and she'd 'ave me up for it as soon as look at me. She's got 'eaps and 'eaps of love-letters o' mine."

" Love-letters ! " ses Alf, staring. " Love-letters when you live in the same house ! "

" She started it," ses his uncle; " she pushed one under my door one morning, and I 'ad to answer it. She wouldn't come down and get my breakfast till I did. I have to send her one every morning."

" Do you sign 'em with your own name ? " ses Alf, arter thinking a bit.

" No," ses 'is uncle, turning red.

" Wot do you sign 'em, then ? " ses Alf.

" Never you mind," ses his uncle, turning redder. " It's my handwriting, and that's good enough for her. I did try writing backwards, but I only did it once. I wouldn't do it agin for fifty pounds. You ought to ha' heard 'er."

"If 'er fust husband was alive she couldn't marry you," ses Alf, very slow and thoughtful.

"No," ses his uncle, nasty-like; "and if I was an old woman she couldn't marry me. You know as well as I do that he went down with the *Evening Star* fifteen years ago."

"So far as she knows," ses Alf; "but there was four of them saved, so why not five? Mightn't 'e have floated away on a spar or something and been picked up? Can't you dream it three nights running, and tell 'er that you feel certain sure he's alive?"

"If I dreamt it fifty times it wouldn't make any difference," ses George Hatchard. "Here! wot are you up to? 'Ave you gone mad, or wot? You poke me in the ribs like that agin if you dare."

"Her fust 'usband's alive," ses Alf, smiling at 'im.

"*Wot?*" ses his uncle.

"He floated away on a bit o' wreckage," ses Alf, nodding at 'im, "just like they do in books, and was picked up more dead than alive and took to Melbourne. He's now living up-country working on a sheep station."

"Who's dreaming now?" ses his uncle.

"It's a fact," ses Alf. "I know a chap wot's

met 'im and talked to 'im. She can't marry you while he's alive, can she?"

"Certainly *not*," ses George Hatchard, trembling all over; "but are you sure you 'aven't made a mistake?"

"Certain sure," ses Alf.

"It's too good to be true," ses George Hatchard.

"O' course it is," ses Alf, "but she won't know that. Look 'ere; you write down all the things that she 'as told you about herself and give it to me, and I'll soon find the chap I spoke of wot's met 'im. He'd meet a dozen men if it was made worth his while."

George Hatchard couldn't understand 'im at fust, and when he did he wouldn't 'ave a hand in it because it wasn't the right thing to do, and because he felt sure that Mrs. Pearce would find it out. But at last 'e wrote out all about her for Alf; her maiden name, and where she was born, and everything; and then he told Alf that, if 'e dared to play such a trick on an unsuspecting, loving woman, he'd never forgive 'im.

"I shall want a couple o' quid," ses Alf.

"Certainly not," ses his uncle. "I won't 'ave nothing to do with it, I tell you."

"Only to buy chocolates with," ses Alf.

"Oh, all right," ses George Hatchard; and he

Alf's Dream

went upstairs to 'is bedroom and came down with three pounds and gave 'im. " If that ain't enough," he ses, " let me know, and you can 'ave more."

Alf winked at 'im, but the old man drew hisself up and stared at 'im, and then 'e turned and walked away with his 'ead in the air.

He 'ardly got a chance of speaking to Alf next day, Mrs. Pearce being 'ere, there, and everywhere, as the saying is, and finding so many little odd jobs for Alf to do that there was no time for talking. But the dar arter he sidled up to 'im when the 'ouse-keeper was out of the room and asked 'im whether he 'ad bought the chocolates.

" Yes," ses Alfred, taking one out of 'is pocket and eating it, " some of 'em."

George Hatchard coughed and fidgeted about. " When are you going to buy the others? " he ses.

" As I want 'em," ses Alf. " They'd spoil if I got 'em all at once."

George Hatchard coughed agin. " I 'ope you haven't been going on with that wicked plan you spoke to me about the other night," he ses.

" Certainly not," ses Alf, winking to 'imself; " not arter wot you said. How could I? "

" That's right," ses the old man. " I'm sorry for this marriage for your sake, Alf. O' course, I was going to leave you my little bit of 'ouse property, but

Alf's Dream

I suppose now it'll 'ave to be left to her. Well, well, I s'pose it's best for a young man to make his own way in the world."

" I s'pose so," ses Alf.

" Mrs. Pearce was asking only yesterday when you was going back to sea agin," ses his uncle, looking at 'im.

" Oh! " ses Alf.

" She's took a dislike to you, I think," ses the old man. " It's very 'ard, my fav'rite nephew, and the only one I've got. I forgot to tell you the other day that her fust 'usband, Charlie Pearce, 'ad a kind of a wart on 'is left ear. She's often spoke to me about it."

" In—deed! " ses Alf.

" Yes," ses his uncle, " *left* ear, and a scar on his forehead where a friend of his kicked 'im one day."

Alf nodded, and then he winked at 'im agin. George Hatchard didn't wink back, but he patted 'im on the shoulder and said 'ow well he was filling out, and 'ow he got more like 'is pore mother every day he lived.

" I 'ad a dream last night," ses Alf. " I dreamt that a man I know named Bill Flurry, but wot called 'imself another name in my dream, and didn't know me then, came 'ere one evening when we was all sitting down at supper, Joe Morgan and 'is missis being

Alf's Dream

"He patted 'im on the shoulder and said 'ow well he was
filling out."

here, and said as 'ow Mrs. Pearce's fust husband was alive and well."

" That's a very odd dream," ses his uncle; " but wot was Joe Morgan and his missis in it for? "

" Witnesses," ses Alf.

George Hatchard fell over a footstool with surprise. " Go on," he ses, rubbing his leg. " It's a queer thing, but I was going to ask the Morgans 'ere to spend the evening next Wednesday."

" Or was it Tuesday? " ses Alf, considering.

" I said Tuesday," ses his uncle, looking over Alf's 'ead so that he needn't see 'im wink agin. " Wot was the end of your dream, Alf? "

" The end of it was," ses Alf, " that you and Mrs. Pearce was both very much upset, as o' course you couldn't marry while 'er fust was alive, and the last thing I see afore I woke up was her boxes standing at the front door waiting for a cab."

George Hatchard was going to ask 'im more about it, but just then Mrs. Pearce came in with a pair of Alf's socks that he 'ad been untidy enough to leave in the middle of the floor instead of chucking 'em under the bed. She was so unpleasant about it that, if it hadn't ha' been for the thought of wot was going to 'appen on Tuesday, Alf couldn't ha' stood it.

For the next day or two George Hatchard was in such a state of nervousness and excitement that

Alf's Dream

Alf was afraid that the 'ousekeeper would notice it. On Tuesday morning he was trembling so much that she said he'd got a chill, and she told 'im to go to bed and she'd make 'im a nice hot mustard poultice. George was afraid to say " no," but while she was in the kitchen making the poultice he slipped out for a walk and cured 'is trembling with three whiskies. Alf nearly got the poultice instead, she was so angry.

She was unpleasant all dinner-time, but she got better in the arternoon, and when the Morgans came in the evening, and she found that Mrs. Morgan 'ad got a nasty sort o' red swelling on her nose, she got quite good-tempered. She talked about it nearly all supper-time, telling 'er what she ought to do to it, and about a friend of hers that 'ad one and 'ad to turn teetotaler on account of it.

" My nose is good enough for me," ses Mrs. Morgan, at last.

" It don't affect 'er appetite," ses George Hatchard, trying to make things pleasant, " and that's the main thing."

Mrs. Morgan got up to go, but arter George Hatchard 'ad explained wot he didn't mean she sat down agin and began to talk to Mrs. Pearce about 'er dress and 'ow beautifully it was made. And she asked Mrs. Pearce to give 'er the pattern of it, because she should 'ave one like it herself when she was old enough. " I do like to see people dressed suitable," she ses, with a smile.

" I think you ought to 'ave a much deeper color than this," ses Mrs. Pearce, considering.

" Not when I'm faded," ses Mrs. Morgan.

Mrs. Pearce, wot was filling 'er glass at the time, spilt a lot of beer all over the tablecloth, and she was so cross about it that she sat like a stone statue for pretty near ten minutes. By the time supper was finished people was passing things to each other in whispers, and when a bit o' cheese went the wrong way with Joe Morgan he nearly suffocated 'imself for fear of making a noise.

They 'ad a game o' cards arter supper, counting twenty nuts as a penny, and everybody got more cheerful. They was all laughing and talking, and Joe Morgan was pretending to steal Mrs. Pearce's nuts, when George Hatchard held up his 'and.

" Somebody at the street door, I think," he ses.

Young Alf got up to open it, and they 'eard a man's voice in the passage asking whether Mrs. Pearce lived there, and the next moment Alf came into the room, followed by Bill Flurry.

" Here's a gentleman o' the name o' Smith asking arter you," he ses, looking at Mrs. Pearce.

" Wot d'you want? " ses Mrs. Pearce rather sharp.

Alf's Dream

" It is 'er," ses Bill, stroking his long white beard and casting 'is eyes up at the ceiling. " You don't remember me, Mrs. Pearce, but I used to see you years ago, when you and poor Charlie Pearce was living down Poplar way."

" Well, wot about it? " ses Mrs. Pearce.

" I'm coming to it," ses Bill Flurry. " I've been two months trying to find you, so there's no need to be in a hurry for a minute or two. Besides, what I've got to say ought to be broke gently, in case you faint away with joy."

" Rubbish! " ses Mrs. Pearce. " I ain't the fainting sort."

" I 'ope it's nothing unpleasant," ses George Hatchard, pouring 'im out a glass of whisky.

" Quite the opposite," ses Bill. " It's the best news she's 'eard for fifteen years."

" Are you going to tell me wot you want, or ain't you? " ses Mrs. Pearce.

" I'm coming to it," ses Bill. " Six months ago I was in Melbourne, and one day I was strolling about looking in at the shop-winders, when all at once I thought I see a face I knew. It was a good bit older than when I see it last, and the whiskers was gray, but I says to myself——"

" I can see wot's coming," ses Mrs. Morgan, turning red with excitement and pinching Joe's arm.

Alf's Dream

"I ses to myself," ses Bill Flurry, "either that's a ghost, I ses or else it's Charlie——"

"Go on," ses George Hatchard, as was sitting with 'is fists clinched on the table and 'is eyes wide open, staring at 'im.

"Pearce," ses Bill Flurry.

You might 'ave heard a pin drop. They all sat staring at 'im, and then George Hatchard took out 'is handkerchief and 'eld it up to 'is face.

"But he was drownded in the *Evening Star*," ses Joe Morgan.

Bill Flurry didn't answer 'im. He poured out pretty near a tumbler of whisky and offered it to Mrs. Pearce, but she pushed it away, and, arter looking round in a 'elpless sort of way and shaking his 'ead once or twice, he finished it up 'imself.

"It couldn't 'ave been 'im," ses George Hatchard, speaking through 'is handkerchief. "I can't believe it. It's too cruel."

"I tell you it was 'im," ses Bill. "He floated off on a spar when the ship went down, and was picked up two days arterwards by a bark and taken to New Zealand. He told me all about it, and he told me if ever I saw 'is wife to give her 'is kind regards."

"*Kind regards!*" ses Joe Morgan, starting up. "Why didn't he let 'is wife know 'e was alive?"

Alf's Dream

" That's wot I said to 'im," ses Bill Flurry; " but he said he 'ad 'is reasons."

" Ah, to be sure," ses Mrs. Morgan, nodding. " Why, you and her can't be married now," she ses, turning to George Hatchard.

" Married? " ses Bill Flurry with a start, as George Hatchard gave a groan that surprised 'imself. " Good gracious! what a good job I found 'er! "

" I s'pose you don't know where he is to be found now? " ses Mrs. Pearce, in a low voice, turning to Bill.

" I do not, ma'am," ses Bill, " but I think you'd find 'im somewhere in Australia. He keeps changing 'is name and shifting about, but I dare say you'd 'ave as good a chance of finding 'im as anybody."

" It's a terrible blow to me," ses George Hatchard, dabbing his eyes.

" I know it is," ses Mrs. Pearce; " but there, you men are all alike. I dare say if this hadn't turned up you'd ha' found something else."

" Oh, 'ow can you talk like that? " ses George Hatchard, very reproachful. " It's the only thing in the world that could 'ave prevented our getting married. I'm surprised at you."

" Well, that's all right, then," ses Mrs. Pearce, " and we'll get married after all."

Alf's Dream

" But you can't," ses Alf.

" It's bigamy," ses Joe Morgan.

" You'd get six months," ses his wife.

" Don't you worry, dear," ses Mrs. Pearce, nodding at George Hatchard; " that man's made a mistake."

" Mistake! " ses Bill Flurry. " Why, I tell you I talked to 'im. It was Charlie Pearce right enough; scar on 'is forehead and a wart on 'is left ear and all."

" It's wonderful," ses Mrs. Pearce. " I can't think where you got it all from."

" Got it all from? " ses Bill, staring at her. " Why, from 'im."

" Oh, of course," ses Mrs. Pearce. " I didn't think of that; but that only makes it the more wonderful, doesn't it?—because, you see, he didn't go on the *Evening Star*."

" *Wot?* " ses George Hatchard. " Why you told me yourself——"

" I know I did," ses Mrs. Pearce, " but that was only just to spare your feelings. Charlie *was* going to sea in her, but he was prevented."

" Prevented? " ses two or three of 'em.

" Yes," ses Mrs. Pearce; " the night afore he was to 'ave sailed there was some silly mistake over a diamond ring, and he got five years. He gave a different name at the police-station, and naturally everybody thought 'e went down with the ship. And when he died in prison I didn't undeceive 'em."

She took out her 'andkerchief, and while she was busy with it Bill Flurry got up and went out on tip-toe. Young Alf got up a second or two arterwards to see where he'd gone; and the last Joe Morgan and his missis see of the happy couple they was sitting on one chair, and George Hatchard was making desprit and 'artrending attempts to smile.

A DISTANT RELATIVE

A Distant Relative

MR. POTTER had just taken Ethel Spriggs into the kitchen to say good-by; in the small front room Mr. Spriggs, with his fingers already fumbling at the linen collar of ceremony, waited impatiently.

"They get longer and longer over their good-bys," he complained.

"It's only natural," said Mrs. Spriggs, looking up from a piece of fine sewing. "Don't you remember——"

"No, I don't," said her husband, doggedly. "I know that your pore father never 'ad to put on a collar for me; and, mind you, I won't wear one after they're married, not if you all went on your bended knees and asked me to."

He composed his face as the door opened, and nodded good-night to the rather over-dressed young man who came through the room with his daughter.

The latter opened the front-door and passing out with Mr. Potter, held it slightly open. A penetrating draught played upon the exasperated Mr. Spriggs. He coughed loudly.

"Your father's got a cold," said Mr. Potter, in a concerned voice.

"No; it's only too much smoking," said the girl. "He's smoking all day long."

The indignant Mr. Spriggs coughed again; but the young people had found a new subject of conversation. It ended some minutes later in a playful scuffle, during which the door acted the part of a ventilating fan.

"It's only for another fortnight," said Mrs. Spriggs, hastily, as her husband rose.

"After they're spliced," said the vindictive Mr. Spriggs, resuming his seat, "I'll go round and I'll play about with their front-door till——"

He broke off abruptly as his daughter, darting into the room, closed the door with a bang that nearly extinguished the lamp, and turned the key. Before her flushed and laughing face Mr. Spriggs held his peace.

"What's the matter?" she asked, eying him. "What are you looking like that for?"

"Too much draught—for your mother," said Mr. Spriggs, feebly. "I'm afraid of her asthma agin."

He fell to work on the collar once more, and, escaping at last from the clutches of that enemy, laid

A Distant Relative

it on the table and unlaced his boots. An attempt to remove his coat was promptly frustrated by his daughter.

" You'll get doing it when you come round to see us," she explained.

Mr. Spriggs sighed, and lighting a short clay pipe —forbidden in the presence of his future son-in-law —fell to watching mother and daughter as they gloated over dress materials and discussed double-widths.

" Anybody who can't be 'appy with her," he said, half an hour later, as his daughter slapped his head by way of bidding him good-night, and retired, " don't deserve to be 'appy."

" I wish it was over," whispered his wife. " She'll break her heart if anything happens, and—and Gussie will be out now in a day or two."

" A gal can't 'elp what her uncle does," said Mr. Spriggs, fiercely; " if Alfred throws her over for that, he's no man."

" Pride is his great fault," said his wife, mournfully.

" It's no good taking up troubles afore they come," observed Mr. Spriggs. " P'r'aps Gussie won't come 'ere."

" He'll come straight here," said his wife, with conviction; " he'll come straight here and try and make a fuss of me, same as he used to do when we was children and I'd got a ha'penny. I know him."

"Cheer up, old gal," said Mr. Spriggs; "if he does, we must try and get rid of 'im; and, if he won't go, we must tell Alfred that he's been to Australia, same as we did Ethel."

His wife smiled faintly.

"That's the ticket," continued Mr. Spriggs. "For one thing, I b'leeve he'll be ashamed to show his face here; but, if he does, he's come back from Australia. See? It'll make it nicer for 'im too. You don't suppose he wants to boast of where he's been?"

"And suppose he comes while Alfred is here?" said his wife.

"Then I say, 'How 'ave you left 'em all in Australia?' and wink at him," said the ready Mr. Spriggs.

"And s'pose you're not here?" objected his wife.

"Then you say it and wink at him," was the reply. "No; I know you can't," he added, hastily, as Mrs. Spriggs raised another objection; "you've been too well brought up. Still, you can try."

It was a slight comfort to Mrs. Spriggs that Mr. Augustus Price did, after all, choose a convenient time for his reappearance. A faint knock sounded on the door two days afterwards as she sat at tea

A Distant Relative

with her husband, and an anxious face with somewhat furtive eyes was thrust into the room.

"Emma!" said a mournful voice, as the upper part of the intruder's body followed the face.

"Gussie!" said Mrs. Spriggs, rising in disorder.

Mr. Price drew his legs into the room, and, closing the door with extraordinary care, passed the cuff of his coat across his eyes and surveyed them tenderly.

"I've come home to die," he said, slowly, and, tottering across the room, embraced his sister with much unction.

"What are you going to die of?" inquired Mr. Spriggs, reluctantly accepting the extended hand.

"Broken 'art, George," replied his brother-in-law, sinking into a chair.

Mr. Spriggs grunted, and, moving his chair a little farther away, watched the intruder as his wife handed him a plate. A troubled glance from his wife reminded him of their arrangements for the occasion, and he cleared his throat several times in vain attempts to begin.

"I'm sorry that we can't ask you to stay with us, Gussie, 'specially as you're so ill," he said, at last; "but p'r'aps you'll be better after picking a bit."

Mr. Price, who was about to take a slice of bread and butter, refrained, and, closing his eyes, uttered a faint moan. " I sha'n't last the night," he muttered.

" That's just it," said Mr. Spriggs, eagerly. " You see, Ethel is going to be married in a fortnight, and if you died here that would put it off."

" I might last longer if I was took care of," said the other, opening his eyes.

" And, besides, Ethel don't know where you've been," continued Mr. Spriggs. " We told 'er that you had gone to Australia. She's going to marry a very partikler young chap—a grocer—and if he found it out it might be awk'ard."

Mr. Price closed his eyes again, but the lids quivered.

" It took 'im some time to get over me being a bricklayer," pursued Mr. Spriggs. " What he'd say to you——"

" Tell 'im I've come back from Australia, if you like," said Mr. Price, faintly. " I don't mind."

Mr. Spriggs cleared his throat again. " But, you see, we told Ethel as you was doing well out there," he said, with an embarrassed laugh, " and girl-like, and Alfred talking a good deal about his relations, she—she's made the most of it."

" It don't matter," said the complaisant Mr. Price; " you say what you like. I sha'n't interfere with you."

A Distant Relative

" But, you see, you don't look as though you've been making money," said his sister, impatiently. " Look at your clothes."

Mr. Price held up his hand. " That's easy got over," he remarked; " while I'm having a bit of tea George can go out and buy me some new ones. You get what you think I should look richest in, George —a black tail-coat would be best, I should think, but I leave it to you. A bit of a fancy waistcoat, p'r'aps, lightish trousers, and a pair o' nice boots, easy sevens."

He sat upright in his chair and, ignoring the look of consternation that passed between husband and wife, poured himself out a cup of tea and took a slice of cake.

" Have you got any money? " said Mr. Spriggs, after a long pause.

" I left it behind me—in Australia," said Mr. Price, with ill-timed facetiousness.

" Getting better, ain't you? " said his brother-in-law, sharply. " How's that broken 'art getting on? "

" It'll go all right under a fancy waistcoat," was the reply; " and while you're about it, George, you'd better get me a scarf-pin, and, if you *could* run to a gold watch and chain——"

He was interrupted by a frenzied outburst from Mr. Spriggs; a somewhat incoherent summary of

A Distant Relative

Mr. Price's past, coupled with unlawful and heathenish hopes for his future.

" You're wasting time," said Mr. Price, calmly, as he paused for breath. " Don't get 'em if you don't want to. I'm trying to help you, that's all. I don't mind anybody knowing where I've been. I was innercent. If you will give way to sinful pride you must pay for it."

Mr. Spriggs, by a great effort, regained his self-control. " Will you go away if I give you a quid? " he asked, quietly.

" No," said Mr. Price, with a placid smile. " I've got a better idea of the value of money than that. Besides, I want to see my dear niece, and see whether that young man's good enough for her."

" Two quid? " suggested his brother-in-law.

Mr. Price shook his head. " I couldn't do it," he said, calmly. " In justice to myself I couldn't do it. You'll be feeling lonely when you lose Ethel, and I'll stay and keep you company."

The bricklayer nearly broke out again; but, obeying a glance from his wife, closed his lips and followed her obediently upstairs. Mr. Price, filling his pipe from a paper of tobacco on the mantelpiece, winked at himself encouragingly in the glass, and smiled gently as he heard the chinking of coins upstairs.

A Distant Relative

"Be careful about the size," he said, as Mr. Spriggs came down and took his hat from a nail; "about a couple of inches shorter than yourself and not near so much round the waist."

Mr. Spriggs regarded him sternly for a few seconds, and then, closing the door with a bang, went off down the street. Left alone, Mr. Price strolled about the room investigating, and then, drawing an easy-chair up to the fire, put his feet on the fender and relapsed into thought.

Two hours later he sat in the same place, a changed and resplendent being. His thin legs were hidden in light check trousers, and the companion waistcoat to Joseph's Coat graced the upper part of his body. A large chrysanthemum in the button-hole of his frock-coat completed the picture of an Australian millionaire, as understood by Mr. Spriggs.

"A nice watch and chain, and a little money in my pockets, and I shall be all right," murmured Mr. Price.

"You won't get any more out o' me," said Mr. Spriggs, fiercely. "I've spent every farthing I've got."

"Except what's in the bank," said his brother-in-law. "It'll take you a day or two to get at it, I know. S'pose we say Saturday for the watch and chain?"

A Distant Relative

Mr. Spriggs looked helplessly at his wife, but she avoided his gaze. He turned and gazed in a fascinated fashion at Mr. Price, and received a cheerful nod in return.

" I'll come with you and help choose it," said the latter. " It'll save you trouble if it don't save your pocket."

He thrust his hands in his trouser-pockets and, spreading his legs wide apart, tilted his head back and blew smoke to the ceiling. He was in the same easy position when Ethel arrived home accompanied by Mr. Potter.

" It's—it's your Uncle Gussie," said Mrs. Spriggs, as the girl stood eying the visitor.

" From Australia," said her husband, thickly.

Mr. Price smiled, and his niece, noticing that he removed his pipe and wiped his lips with the back of his hand, crossed over and kissed his eyebrow. Mr. Potter was then introduced and received a gracious reception, Mr. Price commenting on the extraordinary likeness he bore to a young friend of his who had just come in for forty thousand a year.

" That's nearly as much as you're worth, uncle, isn't it? " inquired Miss Spriggs, daringly.

Mr. Price shook his head at her and pondered. " Rather more," he said, at last, " rather more."

Mr. Potter caught his breath sharply; Mr.

A Distant Relative

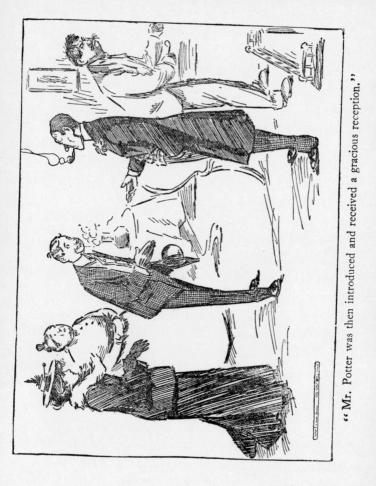

"Mr. Potter was then introduced and received a gracious reception."

A Distant Relative

Spriggs, who was stooping to get a light for his pipe, nearly fell into the fire. There was an impressive silence.

"Money isn't everything," said Mr. Price, looking round and shaking his head. "It's not much good, except to give away."

His eye roved round the room and came to rest finally upon Mr. Potter. The young man noticed with a thrill that it beamed with benevolence.

"Fancy coming over without saying a word to anybody, and taking us all by surprise like this!" said Ethel.

"I felt I must see you all once more before I died," said her uncle, simply. "Just a flying visit I meant it to be, but your father and mother won't hear of my going back just yet."

"Of course not," said Ethel, who was helping the silent Mrs. Spriggs to lay supper.

"When I talked of going your father 'eld me down in my chair," continued the veracious Mr. Price.

"Quite right, too," said the girl. "Now draw your chair up and have some supper, and tell us all about Australia."

Mr. Price drew his chair up, but, as to talking about Australia, he said ungratefully that he was sick of the name of the place, and preferred instead

A Distant Relative

to discuss the past and future of Mr. Potter. He
learned, among other things, that that gentleman was
of a careful and thrifty disposition, and that his savings, augmented by a lucky legacy, amounted to a
hundred and ten pounds.

"Alfred is going to stay with Palmer and Mays
for another year, and then we shall take a business
of our own," said Ethel.

"Quite right," said Mr. Price. "I like to see
young people make their own way," he added mean-
ingly. "It's good for 'em."

It was plain to all that he had taken a great fancy
to Mr. Potter. He discussed the grocery trade with
the air of a rich man seeking a good investment, and
threw out dark hints about returning to England
after a final visit to Australia and settling down in the
bosom of his family. He accepted a cigar from Mr.
Potter after supper, and, when the young man left
—at an unusually late hour—walked home with him.

It was the first of several pleasant evenings, and
Mr. Price, who had bought a book dealing with Australia from a second-hand bookstall, no longer denied them an account of his adventures there. A
gold watch and chain, which had made a serious hole
in his brother-in-law's Savings Bank account, lent
an air of substance to his waistcoat, and a pin of excellent paste sparkled in his neck-tie. Under the in-

fluence of good food and home comforts he improved every day, and the unfortunate Mr. Spriggs was at his wits' end to resist further encroachments. From the second day of their acquaintance he called Mr. Potter " Alf," and the young people listened with great attention to his discourse on " Money: How to Make It and How to Keep It."

His own dealings with Mr. Spriggs afforded an example which he did not quote. Beginning with shillings, he led up to half-crowns, and, encouraged by success, one afternoon boldly demanded a half-sovereign to buy a wedding-present with. Mrs. Spriggs drew her over-wrought husband into the kitchen and argued with him in whispers.

" Give him what he wants till they're married," she entreated; " after that Alfred can't help himself, and it'll be as much to his interest to keep quiet as anybody else."

Mr. Spriggs, who had been a careful man all his life, found the half-sovereign and a few new names, which he bestowed upon Mr. Price at the same time. The latter listened unmoved. In fact, a bright eye and a pleasant smile seemed to indicate that he regarded them rather in the nature of compliments than otherwise.

" I telegraphed over to Australia this morning," he said, as they all sat at supper that evening.

A Distant Relative

"A gold watch and chain lent an air of
substance to his waistcoat."

A Distant Relative

" About my money? " said Mr. Potter, eagerly.

Mr. Price frowned at him swiftly. " No; telling my head clerk to send over a wedding-present for you," he said, his face softening under the eye of Mr. Spriggs. " I've got just the thing for you there. I can't see anything good enough over here."

The young couple were warm in their thanks.

" What did you mean, about your money? " inquired Mr. Spriggs, turning to his future son-in-law.

" Nothing," said the young man, evasively.

" It's a secret," said Mr. Price.

" What about? " persisted Mr. Spriggs, raising his voice.

" It's a little private business between me and Uncle Gussie," said Mr. Potter, somewhat stiffly.

" You—you haven't been lending him money? " stammered the bricklayer.

" Don't be silly, father," said Miss Spriggs, sharply. " What good would Alfred's little bit o' money be to Uncle Gussie? If you must know, Alfred is drawing it out for uncle to invest it for him."

The eyes of Mr. and Mrs. Spriggs and Mr. Price engaged in a triangular duel. The latter spoke first.

" I'm putting it into my business for him," he said, with a threatening glance, " in Australia."

" And he didn't want his generosity known," added Mr. Potter.

A Distant Relative

The bewildered Mr. Spriggs looked helplessly round the table. His wife's foot pressed his, and like a mechanical toy his lips snapped together.

"I didn't know you had got your money handy," said Mrs. Spriggs, in trembling tones.

"I made special application, and I'm to have it on Friday," said Mr. Potter, with a smile. "You don't get a chance like that every day."

He filled Uncle Gussie's glass for him, and that gentleman at once raised it and proposed the health of the young couple. "If anything was to 'appen to break it off now," he said, with a swift glance at his sister, "they'd be miserable for life, I can see that."

"Miserable for ever," assented Mr. Potter, in a sepulchral voice, as he squeezed the hand of Miss Spriggs under the table.

"It's the only thing worth 'aving—love," continued Mr. Price, watching his brother-in-law out of the corner of his eye. "Money is nothing."

Mr. Spriggs emptied his glass and, knitting his brows, drew patterns on the cloth with the back of his knife. His wife's foot was still pressing on his, and he waited for instructions.

For once, however, Mrs. Spriggs had none to give. Even when Mr. Potter had gone and Ethel had retired upstairs she was still voiceless. She sat for some time looking at the fire and stealing an occasional glance at Uncle Gussie as he smoked a cigar; then she arose and bent over her husband.

" Do what you think best," she said, in a weary voice. " Good-night."

" What about that money of young Alfred's? " demanded Mr. Spriggs, as the door closed behind her.

. " I'm going to put it in my business," said Uncle Gussie, blandly; " my business in Australia."

" Ho! You've got to talk to me about that first," said the other.

His brother-in-law leaned back and smoked with placid enjoyment. " You do what you like," he said, easily. " Of course, if you tell Alfred, I sha'n't get the money, and Ethel won't get 'im. Besides that, he'll find out what lies you've been telling."

" I wonder you can look me in the face," said the raging bricklayer.

" And I should give him to understand that you were going shares in the hundred and ten pounds and then thought better of it," said the unmoved Mr. Price. " He's the sort o' young chap as'll believe anything. Bless 'im! "

Mr. Spriggs bounced up from his chair and stood over him with his fists clinched. Mr. Price glared defiance.

" If you're so partikler you can make it up to him,"

he said, slowly. " You've been a saving man, I know, and Emma 'ad a bit left her that I ought to have 'ad. When you've done play-acting I'll go to bed. So long! "

He got up, yawning, and walked to the door, and Mr. Spriggs, after a momentary idea of breaking him in pieces and throwing him out into the street, blew out the lamp and went upstairs to discuss the matter with his wife until morning.

Mr. Spriggs left for his work next day with the question still undecided, but a pretty strong conviction that Mr. Price would have to have his way. The wedding was only five days off, and the house was in a bustle of preparation. A certain gloom which he could not shake off he attributed to a raging toothache, turning a deaf ear to the various remedies suggested by Uncle Gussie, and the name of an excellent dentist who had broken a tooth of Mr. Potter's three times before extracting it.

Uncle Gussie he treated with bare civility in public, and to blood-curdling threats in private. Mr. Price, ascribing the latter to the toothache, also varied his treatment to his company; prescribing whisky held in the mouth, and other agreeable remedies when there were listeners, and recommending him to fill his mouth with cold water and sit on the fire till it boiled, when they were alone.

A Distant Relative

He was at his worst on Thursday morning; on Thursday afternoon he came home a bright and contented man. He hung his cap on the nail with a flourish, kissed his wife, and, in full view of the disapproving Mr. Price, executed a few clumsy steps on the hearthrug.

" Come in for a fortune? " inquired the latter, eying him sourly.

" No; I've saved one," replied Mr. Spriggs, gayly. " I wonder I didn't think of it myself."

" Think of what? " inquired Mr. Price.

" You'll soon know," said Mr. Spriggs, " and you've only got yourself to thank for it."

Uncle Gussie sniffed suspiciously; Mrs. Spriggs pressed for particulars.

" I've got out of the difficulty," said her husband, drawing his chair to the tea-table. " Nobody'll suffer but Gussie."

" Ho! " said that gentleman, sharply.

" I took the day off," said Mr. Spriggs, smiling contentedly at his wife, " and went to see a friend of mine, Bill White the policeman, and told him about Gussie."

Mr. Price stiffened in his chair.

"Acting—under—his—advice," said Mr. Spriggs, sipping his tea, " I wrote to Scotland Yard and told 'em that Augustus Price, ticket-of-leave man, was trying to obtain a hundred and ten pounds by false pretences."

Mr. Price, white and breathless, rose and confronted him.

"The beauty o' that is, as Bill says," continued Mr. Spriggs, with much enjoyment, "that Gussie'll 'ave to set out on his travels again. He'll have to go into hiding, because if they catch him he'll 'ave to finish his time. And Bill says if he writes letters to any of us it'll only make it easier to find him. You'd better take the first train to Australia, Gussie."

"What—what time did you post—the letter?" inquired Uncle Gussie, jerkily.

"'Bout two o'clock," said Mr. Spriggs, glaring at the clock. "I reckon you've just got time."

Mr. Price stepped swiftly to the small sideboard, and, taking up his hat, clapped it on. He paused a moment at the door to glance up and down the street, and then the door closed softly behind him. Mrs. Spriggs looked at her husband.

"Called away to Australia by special telegram," said the latter, winking. "Bill White is a trump; that's what he is."

"Oh, George!" said his wife. "Did you really write that letter?"

Mr. Spriggs winked again.

THE TEST

The Test

PEBBLESEA was dull, and Mr. Frederick Dix, mate of the ketch *Starfish*, after a long and unsuccessful quest for amusement, returned to the harbor with an idea of forgetting his disappointment in sleep. The few shops in the High Street were closed, and the only entertainment offered at the taverns was contained in glass and pewter. The attitude of the landlord of the " Pilots' Hope," where Mr. Dix had sought to enliven the proceedings by a song and dance, still rankled in his memory.

The skipper and the hands were still ashore and the ketch looked so lonely that the mate, thinking better of his idea of retiring, thrust his hands deep in his pockets and sauntered round the harbor. It was nearly dark, and the only other man visible stood at the edge of the quay gazing at the water. He stood for so long that the mate's easily aroused curiosity awoke, and, after twice passing, he edged up to him and ventured a remark on the fineness of the night.

The Test

"The night's all right," said the young man, gloomily.

"You're rather near the edge," said the mate, after a pause.

"I like being near the edge," was the reply.

Mr. Dix whistled softly and, glancing up at the tall, white-faced young man before him, pushed his cap back and scratched his head.

"Ain't got anything on your mind, have you?" he inquired.

The young man groaned and turned away, and the mate, scenting a little excitement, took him gently by the coat-sleeve and led him from the brink. Sympathy begets confidence, and, within the next ten minutes, he had learned that Arthur Heard, rejected by Emma Smith, was contemplating the awful crime of self-destruction.

"Why, I've known 'er for seven years," said Mr. Heard; "seven years, and this is the end of it."

The mate shook his head.

"I told 'er I was coming straight away to drownd myself," pursued Mr. Heard. "My last words to 'er was, 'When you see my bloated corpse you'll be sorry.'"

"I expect she'll cry and carry on like anything," said the mate, politely.

The other turned and regarded him. "Why, you

don't think I'm going to, do you?" he inquired, sharply. "Why, I wouldn't drownd myself for fifty blooming gells."

"But what did you tell her you were going to for, then?" demanded the puzzled mate.

"'Cos I thought it would upset 'er and make 'er give way," said the other, bitterly; "and all it done was to make 'er laugh as though she'd 'ave a fit."

"It would serve her jolly well right if you did drown yourself," said Mr. Dix, judiciously. "It 'ud spoil her life for her."

"Ah, and it wouldn't spoil mine, I s'pose?" rejoined Mr. Heard, with ferocious sarcasm.

"How she will laugh when she sees you to-morrow," mused the mate. "Is she the sort of girl that would spread it about?"

Mr. Heard said that she was, and, forgetting for a moment his great love, referred to her partiality for gossip in the most scathing terms he could muster. The mate, averse to such a tame ending to a promising adventure, eyed him thoughtfully.

"Why not just go in and out again," he said, seductively, "and run to her house all dripping wet?"

"That would be clever, wouldn't it?" said the ungracious Mr. Heard. "Starting to commit sui-

The Test

cide, and then thinking better of it. Why, I should be a bigger laughing-stock than ever."

"But suppose I saved you against your will?" breathed the tempter; "how would that be?"

"It would be all right if I cared to run the risk," said the other, "but I don't. I should look well struggling in the water while you was diving in the wrong places for me, shouldn't I?"

"I wasn't thinking of such a thing," said Mr. Dix, hastily; "twenty strokes is about my mark —with my clothes off. My idea was to pull you out."

Mr. Heard glanced at the black water a dozen feet below. "How?" he inquired, shortly.

"Not here," said the mate. "Come to the end of the quay where the ground slopes to the water. It's shallow there, and you can tell her that you jumped in off here. She won't know the difference."

With an enthusiasm which Mr. Heard made no attempt to share, he led the way to the place indicated, and dilating upon its manifold advantages, urged him to go in at once and get it over.

"You couldn't have a better night for it," he said, briskly. "Why, it makes me feel like a dip myself to look at it."

Mr. Heard gave a surly grunt, and after testing the temperature of the water with his hand, slowly

The Test

and reluctantly immersed one foot. Then, with sudden resolution, he waded in and, ducking his head, stood up gasping.

" Give yourself a good soaking while you're about it," said the delighted mate.

Mr. Heard ducked again, and once more emerging stumbled towards the bank.

" Pull me out," he cried, sharply.

Mr. Dix, smiling indulgently, extended his hands, which Mr. Heard seized with the proverbial grasp of a drowning man.

" All right, take it easy, don't get excited," said the smiling mate, " four foot of water won't hurt anyone. If——Here! Let go o' me, d'ye hear? Let go! If you don't let go I'll punch your head."

" You couldn't save me against my will without coming in," said Mr. Heard. " Now we can tell 'er you dived in off the quay and got me just as I was sinking for the last time. You'll be a hero."

The mate's remarks about heroes were mercifully cut short. He was three stone lighter than Mr. Heard, and standing on shelving ground. The latter's victory was so sudden that he over-balanced, and only a commotion at the surface of the water showed where they had disappeared. Mr. Heard was first up and out, but almost immediately the figure of the mate, who had gone under with his

The Test

mouth open, emerged from the water and crawled ashore.

"You—wait—till I—get my breath back," he gasped.

"There's no ill-feeling, I 'ope?" said Mr. Heard, anxiously. "I'll tell everybody of your bravery. Don't spoil everything for the sake of a little temper."

Mr. Dix stood up and clinched his fists, but at the spectacle of the dripping, forlorn figure before him his wrath vanished and he broke into a hearty laugh.

"Come on, mate," he said, clapping him on the back, "now let's go and find Emma. If she don't fall in love with you now she never will. My eye! you are a picture!"

He began to walk towards the town, and Mr. Heard, with his legs wide apart and his arms held stiffly from his body, waddled along beside him. Two little streamlets followed.

They walked along the quay in silence, and had nearly reached the end of it, when the figure of a man turned the corner of the houses and advanced at a shambling trot towards them.

"Old Smith!" said Mr. Heard, in a hasty whisper. "Now, be careful. Hold me tight."

The new-comer thankfully dropped into a walk

The Test

as he saw them, and came to a standstill with a cry of astonishment as the light of a neighboring lamp revealed their miserable condition.

"Wot, Arthur!" he exclaimed.

"Halloa," said Mr. Heard, drearily.

"The idea o' your being so sinful," said Mr. Smith, severely. "Emma told me wot you said, but I never thought as you'd got the pluck to go and do it. I'm surprised at you."

"I ain't done it," said Mr. Heard, in a sullen voice; "nobody can drown themselves in comfort with a lot of interfering people about."

Mr. Smith turned and gazed at the mate, and a broad beam of admiration shone in his face as he grasped that gentleman's hand.

"Come into the 'ouse both of you and get some dry clothes," he said, warmly.

He thrust his strong, thick-set figure between them, and with a hand on each coat-collar propelled them in the direction of home. The mate muttered something about going back to his ship, but Mr. Smith refused to listen, and stopping at the door of a neat cottage, turned the handle and thrust his dripping charges over the threshold of a comfortable sitting-room.

A pleasant-faced woman of middle age and a pretty girl of twenty rose at their entrance, and a

The Test

faint scream fell pleasantly upon the ears of Mr. Heard.

"Here he is," bawled Mr. Smith; "just saved at the last moment."

"What, two of them?" exclaimed Miss Smith, with a faint note of gratification in her voice. Her gaze fell on the mate, and she smiled approvingly.

"No; this one jumped in and saved 'im," said her father.

"Oh, Arthur!" said Miss Smith. "How could you be so wicked! I never dreamt you'd go and do such a thing—never! I didn't think you'd got it in you."

Mr. Heard grinned sheepishly. "I told you I would," he muttered.

"Don't stand talking here," said Mrs. Smith, gazing at the puddle which was growing in the centre of the carpet; "they'll catch cold. Take 'em upstairs and give 'em some dry clothes. And I'll bring some hot whisky and water up to 'em."

"Rum is best," said Mr. Smith, herding his charges and driving them up the small staircase. "Send young Joe for some. Send up three glasses."

They disappeared upstairs, and Joe appearing at that moment from the kitchen, was hastily sent off to the "Blue Jay" for the rum. A couple of curious

The Test

neighbors helped him to carry it back, and, standing modestly just inside the door, ventured on a few skilled directions as to its preparation. After which, with an eye on Miss Smith, they stood and conversed, mostly in head-shakes.

Stimulated by the rum and the energetic Mr. Smith, the men were not long in changing. Preceded by their host, they came down to the sitting-room again; Mr. Heard with as desperate and unrepentant an air as he could assume, and Mr. Dix trying to conceal his uneasiness by taking great interest in a suit of clothes three sizes too large for him.

" They was both as near drownded as coula oe," said Mr. Smith, looking round; " he ses Arthur fought like a madman to prevent 'imself from being saved."

" It was nothing, really," said the mate, in an almost inaudible voice, as he met Miss Smith's admiring gaze.

" Listen to 'im," said the delighted Mr. Smith; " all brave men are like that. That's wot's made us Englishmen wot we are."

" I don't suppose he knew who it was he was saving," said a voice from the door.

" I didn't want to be saved," said Mr. Heard, defiantly.

The Test

"Well, you can easy do it again, Arthur," said the same voice; "the dock won't run away."

Mr. Heard started and eyed the speaker with same malevolence.

"Tell us all about it," said Miss Smith, gazing at the mate, with her hands clasped. "Did you see him jump in?"

Mr. Dix shook his head and looked at Mr. Heard for guidance. "N—not exactly," he stammered; "I was just taking a stroll round the harbor before turning in, when all of a sudden I heard a cry for help——"

"No you didn't," broke in Mr. Heard, fiercely.

"Well, it sounded like it," said the mate, somewhat taken aback.

"I don't care what it sounded like," said the other. "I didn't say it. It was the last thing I should 'ave called out. I didn't want to be saved."

"P'r'aps he cried 'Emma,'" said the voice from the door.

"Might ha' been that," admitted the mate. "Well, when I heard it I ran to the edge and looked down at the water, and at first I couldn't see anything. Then I saw what I took to be a dog, but, knowing that dogs can't cry 'help!'——"

"Emma," corrected Mr. Heard.

"Emma," said the mate, "I just put my hands

up and dived in. When I came to the surface I struck out for him and tried to seize him from behind, but before I could do so he put his arms round my neck like—like——"

"Like as if it was Emma's," suggested the voice by the door.

Miss Smith rose with majestic dignity and confronted the speaker. "And who asked you in here, George Harris?" she inquired, coldly.

"I see the door open," stammered Mr. Harris—"I see the door open and I thought——"

"If you look again you'll see the handle," said Miss Smith.

Mr. Harris looked, and, opening the door with extreme care, melted slowly from a gaze too terrible for human endurance.

"We went down like a stone," continued the mate, as Miss Smith resumed her seat and smiled at him. "When we came up he tried to get away again. I think we went down again a few more times, but I ain't sure. Then we crawled out; leastways I did, and pulled him after me."

"He might have drowned you," said Miss Smith, with a severe glance at her unfortunate admirer. "And it's my belief that he tumbled in after all, and when you thought he was struggling to get away he was struggling to be saved. That's more like him."

The Test

"Well, they're all right now," said Mr. Smith, as Mr. Heard broke in with some vehemence. "And this chap's going to 'ave the Royal Society's medal for it, or I'll know the reason why."

"No, no," said the mate, hurriedly; "I wouldn't take it, I couldn't think of it."

"Take it or leave it," said Mr. Smith; "but I'm going to the police to try and get it for you. I know the inspector a bit."

"I can't take it," said the horrified mate; "it—it —besides, don't you see, if this isn't kept quiet Mr. Heard will be locked up for trying to commit suicide."

"So he would be," said the other man from his post by the door; "he's quite right."

"And I'd sooner lose fifty medals," said Mr. Dix. "What's the good of me saving him for that?"

A murmur of admiration at the mate's extraordinary nobility of character jarred harshly on the ears of Mr. Heard. Most persistent of all was the voice of Miss Smith, and hardly able to endure things quietly, he sat and watched the tender glances which passed between her and Mr. Dix. Miss Smith, conscious at last of his regards, turned and looked at him.

"You could say you tumbled in, Arthur, and then he would get the medal," she said, softly.

The Test

"*Say!*" shouted the overwrought Mr. Heard. "Say I tum——"

Words failed him. He stood swaying and regarding the company for a moment, and then, flinging open the door, closed it behind him with a bang that made the house tremble.

The mate followed half an hour later, escorted to the ship by the entire Smith family. Fortified by the presence of Miss Smith, he pointed out the exact scene of the rescue without a tremor, and, when her father narrated the affair to the skipper, whom they found sitting on deck smoking a last pipe, listened undismayed to that astonished mariner's comments.

News of the mate's heroic conduct became general the next day, and work on the ketch was somewhat impeded in consequence. It became a point of honor with Mr. Heard's fellow-townsmen to allude to the affair as an accident, but the romantic nature of the transaction was well understood, and full credit given to Mr. Dix for his self-denial in the matter of the medal. Small boys followed him in the street, and half Pebblesea knew when he paid a visit to the Smith's, and discussed his chances. Two nights afterwards, when he and Miss Smith went for a walk in the loneliest spot they could find, conversation turned almost entirely upon the over-crowded condition of the British Isles.

The Test

The *Starfish* was away for three weeks, but the little town no longer looked dull to the mate as she entered the harbor one evening and glided slowly towards her old berth. Emma Smith was waiting to see the ship come in, and his taste for all other amusements had temporarily disappeared.

For two or three days the course of true love ran perfectly smooth; then, like a dark shadow, the figure of Arthur Heard was thrown across its path. It haunted the quay, hung about the house, and cropped up unexpectedly in the most distant solitudes. It came up behind the mate one evening just as he left the ship and walked beside him in silence.

"Halloa," said the mate, at last.

"Halloa," said Mr. Heard. "Going to see Emma?"

"I'm going to see Miss Smith," said the mate.

Mr. Heard laughed; a forced, mirthless laugh.

"And we don't want you following us about," said Mr. Dix, sharply. "If it'll ease your mind, and do you any good to know, you never had a chance. She told me so."

"I sha'n't follow you," said Mr. Heard; "it's your last evening, so you'd better make the most of it."

He turned on his heel, and the mate, pondering on his last words, went thoughtfully on to the house.

The Test

" ' And we don't want you following us about,' said Mr. Dix,
sharply."

The Test

Amid the distraction of pleasant society and a long walk, the matter passed from his mind, and he only remembered it at nine o'clock that evening as a knock sounded on the door and the sallow face of Mr. Heard was thrust into the room.

" Good-evening all," said the intruder.

" Evening, Arthur," said Mr. Smith, affably.

Mr. Heard with a melancholy countenance entered the room and closed the door gently behind him. Then he coughed slightly and shook his head.

" Anything the matter, Arthur? " inquired Mr. Smith, somewhat disturbed by these manifestations.

" I've got something on my mind," said Mr. Heard, with a diabolical glance at the mate—" something wot's been worrying me for a long time. I've been deceiving you."

" That was always your failing, Arthur—deceit-fulness," said Mrs. Smith. " I remember——"

" We've both been deceiving you," interrupted Mr. Heard, loudly. " I didn't jump into the harbor the other night, and I didn't tumble in, and Mr. Fred Dix didn't jump in after me; we just went to the end of the harbor and walked in and wetted our-selves."

There was a moment's intense silence and all eyes turned on the mate. The latter met them boldly.

" It's a habit o' mine to walk into the water and

spoil my clothes for the sake of people I've never met before," he said, with a laugh.

" For shame, Arthur! " said Mr. Smith, with a huge sigh of relief.

" 'Ow can you? " said Mrs. Smith.

" Arthur's been asleep since then," said the mate, still smiling. " All the same, the next time he jumps in he can get out by himself."

Mr. Heard, raising his voice, entered into a minute description of the affair, but in vain. Mr. Smith, rising to his feet, denounced his ingratitude in language which was seldom allowed to pass unchallenged in the presence of his wife, while that lady contributed examples of deceitfulness in the past of Mr. Heard, which he strove in vain to refute. Meanwhile, her daughter patted the mate's hand.

" It's a bit too thin, Arthur," said the latter, with a mocking smile; " try something better next time."

" Very well," said Mr. Heard, in quieter tones; " I dare you to come along to the harbor and jump in, just as you are, where you said you jumped in after me. They'll soon see who's telling the truth."

" He'll do that," said Mr. Smith, with conviction.

For a fraction of a second Mr. Dix hesitated, then, with a steady glance at Miss Smith, he sprang to his feet and accepted the challenge. Mrs. Smith besought him not to be foolish, and, with a vague idea of dissuading him, told him a slanderous anecdote concerning Mr. Heard's aunt. Her daughter gazed at the mate with proud confidence, and, taking his arm, bade her mother to get some dry clothes ready and led the way to the harbor.

The night was fine but dark, and a chill breeze blew up from the sea. Twice the hapless mate thought of backing out, but a glance at Miss Smith's profile and the tender pressure of her arm deterred him. The tide was running out and he had a faint hope that he might keep afloat long enough to be washed ashore alive. He talked rapidly, and his laugh rang across the water. Arrived at the spot they stopped, and Miss Smith looking down into the darkness was unable to repress a shiver.

" Be careful, Fred," she said, laying her hand upon his arm.

The mate looked at her oddly. " All right," he said, gayly, " I'll be out almost before I'm in. You run back to the house and help your mother get the dry clothes ready for me."

His tones were so confident, and his laugh so buoyant, that Mr. Heard, who had been fully expecting him to withdraw from the affair, began to feel that he had under-rated his swimming powers. " Just jumping in and swimming out again is not quite the same as saving a drownding man," he said, with a sneer.

In a flash the mate saw a chance of escape.

" Why, there's no satisfying you," he said, slowly. " If I do go in I can see that you won't own up that you've been lying."

" He'll 'ave to," said Mr. Smith, who, having made up his mind for a little excitement, was in no mind to lose it.

" I don't believe he would," said the mate. " Look here ! " he said, suddenly, as he laid an affectionate arm on the old man's shoulder. " I know what we'll do."

" Well? " said Mr. Smith.

" I'll save *you*," said the mate, with a smile of great relief.

" Save *me?* " said the puzzled Mr. Smith, as his daughter uttered a faint cry. " How? "

" Just as I saved him," said the other, nodding. " You jump in, and after you've sunk twice—same as he did—I'll dive in and save you. At any rate I'll do my best; I promise you I won't come ashore without you."

Mr. Smith hastily flung off the encircling arm and retired a few paces inland. " 'Ave you—ever been —in a lunatic asylum at any time? " he inquired, as soon as he could speak.

The Test

"No," said the mate, gravely.

"Neither 'ave I," said Mr. Smith; "and, what's more, I'm not going."

He took a deep breath and stood simmering. Miss Smith came forward and, with a smothered giggle, took the mate's arm and squeezed it.

"It'll have to be Arthur again, then," said the latter, in a resigned voice.

"*Me?*" cried Mr. Heard, with a start.

"Yes, you!" said the mate, in a decided voice. "After what you said just now I'm not going in without saving somebody. It would be no good. Come on, in you go."

"He couldn't speak fairer than that, Arthur," said Mr. Smith, dispassionately, as he came forward again.

"But I tell you he can't swim," protested Mr. Heard, "not properly. He didn't swim last time; I told you so."

"Never mind; we know what you said," retorted the mate. "All you've got to do is to jump in and I'll follow and save you—same as I did the other night."

"Go on, Arthur," said Mr. Smith, encouragingly. "It ain't cold."

"I tell you he can't swim," repeated Mr. Heard, passionately. "I should be drownded before your eyes."

The Test

" 'I tell you he can't swim,' repeated Mr. Heard, passionately."

"Rubbish," said Mr. Smith. "Why, I believe you're afraid."

"I should be drownded, I tell you," said Mr. Heard. "He wouldn't come in after me."

"Yes, he would," said Mr. Smith, passing a muscular arm round the mate's waist; "'cos the moment you're overboard I'll drop 'im in. Are you ready?"

He stood embracing the mate and waiting, but Mr. Heard, with an infuriated exclamation, walked away. A parting glance showed him that the old man had released the mate, and that the latter was now embracing Miss Smith.

IN THE FAMILY

In the Family

THE oldest inhabitant of Claybury sat beneath the sign of the "Cauliflower" and gazed with affectionate, but dim, old eyes in the direction of the village street.

"No; Claybury men ain't never been much of ones for emigrating," he said, turning to the youthful traveller who was resting in the shade with a mug of ale and a cigarette. "They know they'd 'ave to go a long way afore they'd find a place as 'ud come up to this."

He finished the tablespoonful of beer in his mug and sat for so long with his head back and the inverted vessel on his face that the traveller, who at first thought it was the beginning of a conjuring trick, colored furiously, and asked permission to refill it.

Now and then a Claybury man has gone to foreign parts, said the old man, drinking from the replenished mug, and placing it where the traveller could mark progress without undue strain; but

In the Family

they've, gen'rally speaking, come back and wished as they'd never gone.

The on'y man as I ever heard of that made his fortune by emigrating was Henery Walker's great-uncle, Josiah Walker by name, and he wasn't a Claybury man at all. He made his fortune out o' sheep in Australey, and he was so rich and well-to-do that he could never find time to answer the letters that Henery Walker used to send him when he was hard up.

Henery Walker used to hear of 'im through a relation of his up in London, and tell us all about 'im and his money up at this here " Cauliflower " public-house. And he used to sit and drink his beer and wonder who would 'ave the old man's money arter he was dead.

When the relation in London died Henery Walker left off hearing about his uncle, and he got so worried over thinking that the old man might die and leave his money to strangers that he got quite thin. He talked of emigrating to Australey 'imself, and then, acting on the advice of Bill Chambers—who said it was a cheaper thing to do—he wrote to his uncle instead, and, arter reminding 'im that 'e was an old man living in a strange country, 'e asked 'im to come to Claybury and make his 'ome with 'is loving grand-nephew.

In the Family

It was a good letter, because more than one gave 'im a hand with it, and there was little bits o' Scripture in it to make it more solemn-like. It was wrote on pink paper with pie-crust edges and put in a green envelope, and Bill Chambers said a man must 'ave a 'art of stone if that didn't touch it.

Four months arterwards Henery Walker got an answer to 'is letter from 'is great-uncle. It was a nice letter, and, arter thanking Henery Walker for all his kindness, 'is uncle said that he was getting an old man, and p'r'aps he should come and lay 'is bones in England arter all, and if he did 'e should certainly come and see his grand-nephew, Henery Walker.

Most of us thought Henery Walker's fortune was as good as made, but Bob Pretty, a nasty, low poaching chap that has done wot he could to give Claybury a bad name, turned up his nose at it.

" I'll believe he's coming 'ome when I see him," he ses. " It's my belief he went to Australey to get out o' your way, Henery."

" As it 'appened he went there afore I was born," ses Henery Walker, firing up.

" He knew your father," ses Bob Pretty, " and he didn't want to take no risks."

They 'ad words then, and arter that every time Bob Pretty met 'im he asked arter his great-uncle's

155

In the Family

'ealth, and used to pretend to think 'e was living with 'im.

"You ought to get the old gentleman out a bit more, Henery," he would say; "it can't be good for 'im to be shut up in the 'ouse so much—especially your 'ouse."

Henery Walker used to get that riled he didn't know wot to do with 'imself, and as time went on, and he began to be afraid that 'is uncle never would come back to England, he used to get quite nasty if anybody on'y so much as used the word "uncle" in 'is company.

It was over six months since he 'ad had the letter from 'is uncle, and 'e was up here at the "Cauliflower" with some more of us one night, when Dicky Weed, the tailor, turns to Bob Pretty and he ses, "Who's the old gentleman that's staying with you, Bob?"

Bob Pretty puts down 'is beer very careful and turns round on 'im.

"Old gentleman?" he ses, very slow. "Wot are you talking about?"

"I mean the little old gentleman with white whiskers and a squeaky voice," ses Dicky Weed.

"You've been dreaming," ses Bob, taking up 'is beer ag'in.

"I see 'im too, Bob," ses Bill Chambers.

In the Family

"Ho, you did, did you?" ses Bob Pretty, putting down 'is mug with a bang. "And wot d'ye mean by coming spying round my place, eh? Wot d'ye mean by it?"

"Spying?" ses Bill Chambers, gaping at 'im with 'is mouth open; "I wasn't spying. Anyone 'ud think you 'ad done something you was ashamed of."

"You mind your business and I'll mind mine," ses Bob, very fierce.

"I was passing the 'ouse," ses Bill Chambers, looking round at us, "and I see an old man's face at the bedroom winder, and while I was wondering who 'e was a hand come and drawed 'im away. I see 'im as plain as ever I see anything in my life, and the hand, too. Big and dirty it was."

"And he's got a cough," ses Dicky Weed—"a churchyard cough—I 'eard it."

"It ain't much you don't hear, Dicky," ses Bob Pretty, turning on 'im; "the on'y thing you never did 'ear, and never will 'ear, is any good of yourself."

He kicked over a chair wot was in 'is way and went off in such a temper as we'd never seen 'im in afore, and, wot was more surprising still, but I know it's true, 'cos I drunk it up myself, he'd left over arf a pint o' beer in 'is mug.

In the Family

"He's up to something," ses Sam Jones, starting arter him; "mark my words."

We couldn't make head nor tail out of it, but for some days arterward you'd ha' thought that Bob Pretty's 'ouse was a peep-show. Everybody stared at the winders as they went by, and the children played in front of the 'ouse and stared in all day long. Then the old gentleman was seen one day as bold as brass sitting at the winder, and we heard that it was a pore old tramp Bob Pretty 'ad met on the road and given a home to, and he didn't like 'is good-'artedness to be known for fear he should be made fun of.

Nobody believed that, o' course, and things got more puzzling than ever. Once or twice the old gentleman went out for a walk, but Bob Pretty or 'is missis was always with 'im, and if anybody tried to speak to him they always said 'e was deaf and took 'im off as fast as they could. Then one night up at the "Cauliflower" here Dicky Weed came rushing in with a bit o' news that took everybody's breath away.

"I've just come from the post-office," he ses, "and there's a letter for Bob Pretty's old gentleman! Wot d'ye think o' that?"

"If you could tell us wot's inside it you might 'ave something to brag about," ses Henery Walker.

158

In the Family

"I don't want to see the inside," ses Dicky Weed; "the name on the outside was good enough for me. I couldn't hardly believe my own eyes, but there it was: 'Mr. Josiah Walker,' as plain as the nose on your face."

O' course, we see it all then, and wondered why we hadn't thought of it afore; and we stood quiet listening to the things that Henery Walker said about a man that would go and steal another man's great-uncle from 'im. Three times Smith, the landlord, said, "*Hush!*" and the fourth time he put Henery Walker outside and told 'im to stay there till he 'ad lost his voice.

Henery Walker stayed outside five minutes, and then 'e come back in ag'in to ask for advice. His idea seemed to be that, as the old gentleman was deaf, Bob Pretty was passing 'isself off as Henery Walker, and the disgrace was a'most more than 'e could bear. He began to get excited ag'in, and Smith 'ad just said "*Hush!*" once more when we 'eard somebody whistling outside, and in come Bob Pretty.

He 'ad hardly got 'is face in at the door afore Henery Walker started on 'im, and Bob Pretty stood there, struck all of a heap, and staring at 'im as though he couldn't believe his ears.

"'Ave you gone mad, Henery?" he ses, at last.

In the Family

"Give me back my great-uncle," ses Henery Walker, at the top of 'is voice.

Bob Pretty shook his 'ead at him. "I haven't got your great-uncle, Henery," he ses, very gentle. "I know the name is the same, but wot of it? There's more than one Josiah Walker in the world. This one is no relation to you at all; he's a very respectable old gentleman."

"I'll go and ask 'im," ses Henery Walker, getting up, "and I'll tell 'im wot sort o' man you are, Bob Pretty."

"He's gone to bed now, Henery," ses Bob Pretty.

"I'll come in the fust thing to-morrow morning, then," ses Henery Walker.

"Not in my 'ouse, Henery," ses Bob Pretty; "not arter the things you've been sayin' about me. I'm a pore man, but I've got my pride. Besides, I tell you he ain't your uncle. He's a pore old man I'm giving a 'ome to, and I won't 'ave 'im worried."

"'Ow much does 'e pay you a week, Bob?" ses Bill Chambers.

Bob Pretty pretended not to hear 'im.

"Where did your wife get the money to buy that bonnet she 'ad on on Sunday?" ses Bill Chambers. "My wife ses it's the fust new bonnet she has 'ad since she was married."

In the Family

"And where did the new winder curtains come from?" ses Peter Gubbins.

Bob Pretty drank up 'is beer and stood looking at them very thoughtful; then he opened the door and went out without saying a word.

"He's got your great-uncle a prisoner in his 'ouse, Henery," ses Bill Chambers; "it's easy for to see that the pore old gentleman is getting past things, and I shouldn't wonder if Bob Pretty don't make 'im leave all 'is money to 'im."

Henery Walker started raving ag'in, and for the next few days he tried his 'ardest to get a few words with 'is great-uncle, but Bob Pretty was too much for 'im. Everybody in Claybury said wot a shame it was, but it was all no good, and Henery Walker used to leave 'is work and stand outside Bob Pretty's for hours at a time in the 'opes of getting a word with the old man.

He got 'is chance at last, in quite a unexpected way. We was up 'ere at the "Cauliflower" one evening, and, as it 'appened, we was talking about Henery Walker's great-uncle, when the door opened, and who should walk in but the old gentleman 'imself. Everybody left off talking and stared at 'im, but he walked up to the bar and ordered a glass o' gin and beer as comfortable as you please.

In the Family

Bill Chambers was the fust to get 'is presence of mind back, and he set off arter Henery Walker as fast as 'is legs could carry 'im, and in a wunnerful short time, considering, he came back with Henery, both of 'em puffing and blowing their 'ardest.

" There—he—is! " ses Bill Chambers, pointing to the old gentleman.

Henery Walker gave one look, and then 'e slipped over to the old man and stood all of a tremble, smiling at 'im. " Good-evening," he ses.

" Wot? " ses the old gentleman.

" Good-evening! " ses Henery Walker ag'in.

" I'm a bit deaf," ses the old gentleman, putting his 'and to his ear.

" GOOD-EVENING! " ses Henery Walker ag'in, shouting. " I'm your grand-nephew, Henery Walker! "

" Ho, are you? " ses the old gentleman, not at all surprised. " Bob Pretty was telling me all about you."

" I 'ope you didn't listen to 'im," ses Henery Walker, all of a tremble. " Bob Pretty'd say anything except his prayers."

" He ses you're arter my money," ses the old gentleman, looking at 'im.

" He's a liar, then," ses Henery Walker; " he's

162

In the Family

arter it 'imself. And it ain't a respectable place for you to stay at. Anybody'll tell you wot a rascal Bob Pretty is. Why, he's a byword."

"Everybody is arter my money," ses the old gentleman, looking round. "Everybody."

"I 'ope you'll know me better afore you've done with me, uncle," ses Henery Walker, taking a seat alongside of 'im. "Will you 'ave another mug o' beer?"

"Gin and beer," ses the old gentleman, cocking his eye up very fierce at Smith, the landlord; "and mind the gin don't get out ag'in, same as it did in the last."

Smith asked 'im wot he meant, but 'is deafness come on ag'in. Henery Walker 'ad an extra dose o' gin put in, and arter he 'ad tasted it the old gentleman seemed to get more amiable-like, and 'im and Henery Walker sat by theirselves talking quite comfortable.

"Why not come and stay with me?" ses Henery Walker, at last. "You can do as you please and have the best of everything."

"Bob Pretty ses you're arter my money," ses the old gentleman, shaking his 'ead. "I couldn't trust you."

"He ses that to put you ag'in me," ses Henery Walker, pleading-like.

In the Family

"Well, wot do you want me to come and live with you for, then?" ses old Mr. Walker.

"Because you're my great-uncle," ses Henery Walker, "and my 'ouse is the proper place for you. Blood is thicker than water."

"And you don't want my money?" ses the old man, looking at 'im very sharp.

"Certainly not," ses Henery Walker.

"And 'ow much 'ave I got to pay a week?" ses old Mr. Walker. "That's the question?"

"Pay?" ses Henery Walker, speaking afore he 'ad time to think. "Pay? Why, I don't want you to pay anything."

The old gentleman said as 'ow he'd think it over, and Henery started to talk to 'im about his father and an old aunt named Maria, but 'e stopped 'im sharp, and said he was sick and tired of the whole Walker family, and didn't want to 'ear their names ag'in as long as he lived. Henery Walker began to talk about Australey then, and asked 'im 'ow many sheep he'd got, and the words was 'ardly out of 'is mouth afore the old gentleman stood up and said he was arter his money ag'in.

Henery Walker at once gave 'im some more gin and beer, and arter he 'ad drunk it the old gentleman said that he'd go and live with 'im for a little while to see 'ow he liked it.

In the Family

"'You leave go o' my lodger,' ses Bob Pretty."

In the Family

"But I sha'n't pay anything," he ses, very sharp; "mind that."

"I wouldn't take it if you offered it to me," ses Henery Walker. "You'll come straight 'ome with me to-night, won't you?"

Afore old Mr. Walker could answer the door opened and in came Bob Pretty. He gave one look at Henery Walker and then he walked straight over to the old gentleman and put his 'and on his shoulder.

"Why, I've been looking for you everywhere, Mr. Walker," he ses. "I couldn't think wot had 'appened to you."

"You needn't worry yourself, Bob," ses Henery Walker; "he's coming to live with me now."

"Don't you believe it," ses Bob Pretty, taking hold of old Mr. Walker by the arm; "he's my lodger, and he's coming with me."

He began to lead the old gentleman towards the door, but Henery Walker, wot was still sitting down, threw 'is arms round his legs and held 'im tight. Bob Pretty pulled one way and Henery Walker pulled the other, and both of 'em shouted to each other to leave go. The row they made was awful, but old Mr. Walker made more noise than the two of 'em put together.

"You leave go o' my lodger," ses Bob Pretty.

"You leave go o' my great-uncle—my dear great-

In the Family

uncle," ses Henery Walker, as the old gentleman called 'im a bad name and asked 'im whether he thought he was made of iron.

I believe they'd ha' been at it till closing-time, on'y Smith, the landlord, came running in from the back and told them to go outside. He 'ad to shout to make 'imself heard, and all four of 'em seemed to be trying which could make the most noise.

"He's my lodger," ses Bob Pretty, "and he can't go without giving me proper notice; that's the lor— a week's notice."

They all shouted ag'in then, and at last the old gentleman told Henery Walker to give Bob Pretty ten shillings for the week's notice and ha' done with 'im. Henery Walker 'ad only got four shillings with 'im, but 'e borrowed the rest from Smith, and arter he 'ad told Bob Pretty wot he thought of 'im he took old Mr. Walker by the arm and led him 'ome a'most dancing for joy.

Mrs. Walker was nearly as pleased as wot 'e was, and the fuss they made of the old gentleman was sinful a'most. He 'ad to speak about it 'imself at last, and he told 'em plain that when 'e wanted arf-a-dozen sore-eyed children to be brought down in their night-gowns to kiss 'im while he was eating sausages, he'd say so.

Arter that Mrs. Walker was afraid that 'e might

In the Family

object when her and her 'usband gave up their bed-room to 'im; but he didn't. He took it all as 'is right, and when Henery Walker, who was sleeping in the next room with three of 'is boys, fell out o' bed for the second time, he got up and rapped on the wall.

Bob Pretty came round the next morning with a tin box that belonged to the old man, and 'e was so perlite and nice to 'im that Henery Walker could see that he 'ad 'opes of getting 'im back ag'in. The box was carried upstairs and put under old Mr. Walker's bed, and 'e was so partikler about its being locked, and about nobody being about when 'e opened it, that Mrs. Walker went arf out of her mind with curi-osity.

" I s'pose you've looked to see that Bob Pretty didn't take anything out of it? " ses Henery Walker.

" He didn't 'ave the chance," ses the old gentle-man. " It's always kep' locked."

" It's a box that looks as though it might 'ave been made in Australey," ses Henery Walker, who was longing to talk about them parts.

" If you say another word about Australey to me," ses old Mr. Walker, firing up, " off I go. Mind that! You're arter my money, and if you're not careful you sha'n't 'ave a farthing of it."

That was the last time the word " Australey "

In the Family

passed Henery Walker's lips, and even when 'e saw his great-uncle writing letters there he didn't say anything. And the old man was so suspicious of Mrs. Walker's curiosity that all the letters that was wrote to 'im he 'ad sent to Bob Pretty's. He used to call there pretty near every morning to see whether any 'ad come for 'im.

In three months Henery Walker 'adn't seen the color of 'is money once, and, wot was worse still, he took to giving Henery's things away. Mrs. Walker 'ad been complaining for some time of 'ow bad the hens had been laying, and one morning at breakfast-time she told her 'usband that, besides missing eggs, two of 'er best hens 'ad been stolen in the night.

"They wasn't stolen," ses old Mr. Walker, putting down 'is teacup. "I took 'em round this morning and give 'em to Bob Pretty."

"Give 'em to Bob Pretty?" ses Henery Walker, arf choking. "Wot for?"

"'Cos he asked me for 'em," ses the old gentleman. "Wot are you looking at me like that for?"

Henery couldn't answer 'im, and the old gentleman, looking very fierce, got up from the table and told Mrs. Walker to give 'im his hat. Henery Walker clung to 'im with tears in his eyes a'most and begged 'im not to go, and arter a lot of talk old

In the Family

Mr. Walker said he'd look over it this time, but it mustn't occur ag'in.

Arter that 'e did as 'e liked with Henery Walker's things, and Henery dursen't say a word to 'im. Bob Pretty used to come up and flatter 'im and beg 'im to go back and lodge with 'im, and Henery was so afraid he'd go that he didn't say a word when old Mr. Walker used to give Bob Pretty things to make up for 'is disappointment. He 'eard on the quiet from Bill Chambers, who said that the old man 'ad told it to Bob Pretty as a dead secret, that 'e 'ad left 'im all his money, and he was ready to put up with anything.

The old man must ha' been living with Henery Walker for over eighteen months when one night he passed away in 'is sleep. Henery knew that his 'art was wrong, because he 'ad just paid Dr. Green 'is bill for saying that 'e couldn't do anything for 'im, but it was a surprise to 'im all the same. He blew his nose 'ard and Mrs. Walker kept rubbing 'er eyes with her apron while they talked in whispers and wondered 'ow much money they 'ad come in for.

In less than ten minutes the news was all over Claybury, and arf the people in the place hanging round in front of the 'ouse waiting to hear 'ow much the Walkers 'ad come in for. Henery Walker pulled the blind on one side for a moment and shook his

In the Family

'ead at them to go away. Some of them did go back
a yard or two, and then they stood staring at Bob
Pretty, wot come up as bold as brass and knocked at
the door.

"Wot's this I 'ear?" he ses, when Henery Walker
opened it. "You don't mean to tell me that the pore
old gentleman has really gone? I told 'im wot would
happen if 'e came to lodge with you."

"You be off," ses Henery Walker; "he hasn't
left you anything."

"I know that," ses Bob Pretty, shaking his 'ead.
"You're welcome to it, Henery, if there is anything.
I never bore any malice to you for taking of 'im
away from us. I could see you'd took a fancy to
'im from the fust. The way you pretended 'e was
your great-uncle showed me that."

"Wot are you talking about?" ses Henery
Walker. "He *was* my great-uncle!"

"Have it your own way, Henery," ses Bob Pretty;
"on'y, if you asked me, I should say that he was my
wife's grandfather."

"*Your — wife's — grandfather?*" ses Henery
Walker, in a choking voice.

He stood staring at 'im, stupid-like, for a minute
or two, but he couldn't get out another word. In a
flash 'e saw 'ow he'd been done, and how Bob Pretty
'ad been deceiving 'im all along, and the idea that

In the Family

" He slammed the door in Bob Pretty's face."

In the Family

he 'ad arf ruined himself keeping Mrs. Pretty's grandfather for 'em pretty near sent 'im out of his mind.

"But how is it 'is name was Josiah Walker, same as Henery's great-uncle?" ses Bill Chambers, who 'ad been crowding round with the others. "Tell me that!"

"He 'ad a fancy for it," ses Bob Pretty, "and being a 'armless amusement we let him 'ave his own way. I told Henery Walker over and over ag'in that it wasn't his uncle, but he wouldn't believe me. I've got witnesses to it. Wot did you say, Henery?"

Henery Walker drew 'imself up as tall as he could and stared at him. Twice he opened 'is mouth to speak but couldn't, and then he made a odd sort o' choking noise in his throat, and slammed the door in Bob Pretty's face.

A LOVE-KNOT

A Love-Knot

MR. NATHANIEL CLARK and Mrs. Bowman had just finished their third game of draughts. It had been a difficult game for Mr. Clark, the lady's mind having been so occupied with other matters that he had had great difficulty in losing. Indeed, it was only by pushing an occasional piece of his own off the board that he had succeeded.

"A penny for your thoughts, Amelia," he said, at last.

Mrs. Bowman smiled faintly. "They were far away," she confessed.

Mr. Clark assumed an expression of great solemnity; allusions of this kind to the late Mr. Bowman were only too frequent. He was fortunate when they did not grow into reminiscences of a career too blameless for successful imitation.

"I suppose," said the widow, slowly—"I suppose I ought to tell you: I've had a letter."

Mr. Clark's face relaxed.

"It took me back to the old scenes," continued Mrs. Bowman, dreamily. "I have never kept anything back from you, Nathaniel. I told you all about the first man I ever thought anything of—Charlie Tucker?"

Mr. Clark cleared his throat. "You did," he said, a trifle hoarsely. "More than once."

"I've just had a letter from him," said Mrs. Bowman, simpering. "Fancy, after all these years! Poor fellow, he has only just heard of my husband's death, and, by the way he writes——"

She broke off and drummed nervously on the table.

"He hasn't heard about me, you mean," said Mr. Clark, after waiting to give her time to finish.

"How should he?" said the widow.

"If he heard one thing, he might have heard the other," retorted Mr. Clark. "Better write and tell him. Tell him that in six weeks' time you'll be Mrs. Clark. Then, perhaps, he won't write again."

Mrs. Bowman sighed. "I thought, after all these years, that he must be dead," she said, slowly, "or else married. But he says in his letter that he has kept single for my sake all these years."

"Well, he'll be able to go on doing it," said Mr.

A Love-Knot

Clark; " it'll come easy to him after so much practice."

" He—he says in his letter that he is coming to see me," said the widow, in a low voice, " to—to—this evening."

" Coming to see you?" repeated Mr. Clark, sharply. " What for?"

" To talk over old times, he says," was the reply. " I expect he has altered a great deal; he was a fine-looking fellow—and so dashing. After I gave him up he didn't care what he did. The last I heard of him he had gone abroad."

Mr. Clark muttered something under his breath, and, in a mechanical fashion, began to build little castles with the draughts. He was just about to add to an already swaying structure when a thundering rat-tat-tat at the door dispersed the draughts to the four corners of the room. The servant opened the door, and the next moment ushered in Mrs. Bowman's visitor.

A tall, good-looking man in a frock-coat, with a huge spray of mignonette in his button-hole, met the critical gaze of Mr. Clark. He paused at the door and, striking an attitude, pronounced in tones of great amazement the Christian name of the lady of the house.

" Mr. Tucker!" said the widow, blushing.

"The same girl," said the visitor, looking round wildly, "the same as the day she left me. Not a bit changed; not a hair different."

He took her extended hand and, bending over it, kissed it respectfully.

"It's—it's very strange to see you again, Mr. Tucker," said Mrs. Bowman, withdrawing her hand in some confusion.

"Mr. Tucker!" said that gentleman, reproachfully; "it used to be Charlie."

Mrs. Bowman blushed again, and, with a side glance at the frowning Mr. Clark, called her visitor's attention to him and introduced them. The gentlemen shook hands stiffly.

"Any friend of yours is a friend of mine," said Mr. Tucker, with a patronizing air. "How are you, sir?"

Mr. Clark replied that he was well, and, after some hesitation, said that he hoped he was the same. Mr. Tucker took a chair and, leaning back, stroked his huge mustache and devoured the widow with his eyes. "Fancy seeing you again!" said the latter, in some embarrassment. "How did you find me out?"

"It's a long story," replied the visitor, "but I always had the idea that we should meet again. Your photograph has been with me all over the world. In the backwoods of Canada, in the bush of Austra-

A Love-Knot

lia, it has been my one comfort and guiding star. If ever I was tempted to do wrong, I used to take your photograph out and look at it."

" I s'pose you took it out pretty often? " said Mr. Clark, restlessly. " To look at, I mean," he added, hastily, as Mrs. Bowman gave him an indignant glance.

" Every day," said the visitor, solemnly. " Once when I injured myself out hunting, and was five days without food or drink, it was the only thing that kept me alive."

Mr. Clark's gibe as to the size of the photograph was lost in Mrs. Bowman's exclamations of pity.

" *I* once lived on two ounces of gruel and a cup of milk a day for ten days," he said, trying to catch the widow's eye. " After the ten days——"

" When the Indians found me I was delirious," continued Mr. Tucker, in a hushed voice, " and when I came to my senses I found that they were calling me ' Amelia.' "

Mr. Clark attempted to relieve the situation by a jocose inquiry as to whether he was wearing a mustache at the time, but Mrs. Bowman frowned him down. He began to whistle under his breath, and Mrs. Bowman promptly said, " *H'sh!* "

" But how did you discover me? " she inquired, turning again to the visitor.

" Wandering over the world," continued Mr. Tucker, " here to-day and there to-morrow, and unable to settle down anywhere, I returned to Northtown about two years ago. Three days since, in a tramcar, I heard your name mentioned. I pricked up my ears and listened; when I heard that you were free I could hardly contain myself. I got into conversation with the lady and obtained your address, and after travelling fourteen hours here I am."

" How very extraordinary ! " said the widow. " I wonder who it could have been? Did she mention her name? "

Mr. Tucker shook his head. Inquiries as to the lady's appearance, age, and dress were alike fruitless. " There was a mist before my eyes," he explained. " I couldn't realize it. I couldn't believe in my good fortune."

" I can't think——" began Mrs. Bowman.

" What does it matter? " inquired Mr. Tucker, softly. " Here we are together again, with life all before us and the misunderstandings of long ago all forgotten."

Mr. Clark cleared his throat preparatory to speech, but a peremptory glance from Mrs. Bowman restrained him.

" I thought you were dead," she said, turning to

the smiling Mr. Tucker. " I never dreamed of seeing you again."

" Nobody would," chimed in Mr. Clark. " When do you go back? "

" Back? " said the visitor. " Where? "

" Australia," replied Mr. Clark, with a glance of defiance at the widow. " You must ha' been missed a great deal all this time."

Mr. Tucker regarded him with a haughty stare. Then he bent towards Mrs. Bowman.

" Do you wish me to go back? " he asked, impressively.

" We don't wish either one way or the other," said Mr. Clark, before the widow could speak. " It don't matter to us."

" We? " said Mr. Tucker, knitting his brows and gazing anxiously at Mrs. Bowman. " *We?* "

" We are going to be married in six weeks' time," said Mr. Clark.

Mr. Tucker looked from one to the other in silent misery; then, shielding his eyes with his hand, he averted his head. Mrs. Bowman, with her hands folded in her lap, regarded him with anxious solicitude.

" I thought perhaps you ought to know," said Mr. Clark.

Mr. Tucker sat bolt upright and gazed at him

fixedly. " I wish you joy," he said, in a hollow voice.

" Thankee," said Mr. Clark; " we expect to be pretty happy." He smiled at Mrs. Bowman, but she made no response. Her looks wandered from one to the other—from the good-looking, interesting companion of her youth to the short, prosaic little man who was exulting only too plainly in his discomfiture.

Mr. Tucker rose with a sigh. " Good-by," he said, extending his hand.

" You are not going—yet? " said the widow.

Mr. Tucker's low-breathed " I must " was just audible. The widow renewed her expostulations.

" Perhaps he has got a train to catch," said the thoughtful Mr. Clark.

" No, sir," said Mr. Tucker. " As a matter of fact, I had taken a room at the George Hotel for a week, but I suppose I had better get back home again."

" No; why should you? " said Mrs. Bowman, with a rebellious glance at Mr. Clark. " Stay, and come in and see me sometimes and talk over old times. And Mr. Clark will be glad to see you, I'm sure. Won't you Nath—Mr. Clark? "

" I shall be—delighted," said Mr. Clark, staring hard at the mantelpiece. " De-lighted."

A Love-Knot

"On the third morning he took Mrs. Bowman out for a walk."

A Love-Knot

Mr. Tucker thanked them both, and after groping for some time for the hand of Mr. Clark, who was still intent upon the mantelpiece, pressed it warmly and withdrew. Mrs. Bowman saw him to the door, and a low-voiced colloquy, in which Mr. Clark caught the word " afternoon," ensued. By the time the widow returned to the room he was busy building with the draughts again.

Mr. Tucker came the next day at three o'clock, and the day after at two. On the third morning he took Mrs. Bowman out for a walk, airily explaining to Mr. Clark, who met them on the way, that they had come out to call for him. The day after, when Mr. Clark met them returning from a walk, he was assured that his silence of the day before was understood to indicate a distaste for exercise.

" And, you see, I like a long walk," said Mrs. Bowman, " and you are not what I should call a good walker."

" You never used to complain," said Mr. Clark; " in fact, it was generally you that used to suggest turning back."

" She wants to be amused as well," remarked Mr. Tucker; " then she doesn't feel the fatigue."

Mr. Clark glared at him, and then, shortly declining Mrs. Bowman's invitation to accompany them home, on the ground that he required exercise,

A Love-Knot

proceeded on his way. He carried himself so stiffly, and his manner was so fierce, that a well-meaning neighbor who had crossed the road to join him, and offer a little sympathy if occasion offered, talked of the weather for five minutes and inconsequently faded away at a corner.

Trimington as a whole watched the affair with amusement, although Mr. Clark's friends adopted an inflection of voice in speaking to him which reminded him strongly of funerals. Mr. Tucker's week was up, but the landlord of the George was responsible for the statement that he had postponed his departure indefinitely.

Matters being in this state, Mr. Clark went round to the widow's one evening with the air of a man who has made up his mind to decisive action. He entered the room with a bounce and, hardly deigning to notice the greeting of Mr. Tucker, planted himself in a chair and surveyed him grimly. "I thought I should find you here," he remarked.

"Well, I always am here, ain't I?" retorted Mr. Tucker, removing his cigar and regarding him with mild surprise.

"Mr. Tucker is my friend," interposed Mrs. Bowman. "I am the only friend he has got in Trimington. It's natural he should be here."

Mr. Clark quailed at her glance.

A Love-Knot

"People are beginning to talk," he muttered, feebly.

"Talk?" said the widow, with an air of mystification belied by her color. "What about?"

Mr. Clark quailed again. "About—about our wedding," he stammered.

Mr. Tucker and the widow exchanged glances. Then the former took his cigar from his mouth and, with a hopeless gesture threw it into the grate.

"Plenty of time to talk about that," said Mrs. Bowman, after a pause.

"Time is going," remarked Mr. Clark. "I was thinking, if it was agreeable to you, of putting up the banns to-morrow."

"There—there's no hurry," was the reply.

"'Marry in haste, repent at leisure,'" quoted Mr. Tucker, gravely.

"Don't you want me to put 'em up?" demanded Mr. Clark, turning to Mrs. Bowman.

"There's no hurry," said Mrs. Bowman again. "I—I want time to think."

Mr. Clark rose and stood over her, and after a vain attempt to meet his gaze she looked down at the carpet.

"I understand," he said, loftily. "I am not blind."

"It isn't my fault," murmured the widow, draw-

A Love-Knot

ing patterns with her toe on the carpet. "One can't help their feelings."

Mr. Clark gave a short, hard laugh. "What about my feelings?" he said, severely. "What about the life you have spoiled? I couldn't have believed it of you."

"I'm sure I'm very sorry," murmured Mrs. Bowman, "and anything that I can do I will. I never expected to see Charles again. And it was so sudden; it took me unawares. I hope we shall still be friends."

"Friends!" exclaimed Mr. Clark, with extraordinary vigor. "With *him?*"

He folded his arms and regarded the pair with a bitter smile; Mrs. Bowman, quite unable to meet his eyes, still gazed intently at the floor.

"You have made me the laughing-stock of Trimington," pursued Mr. Clark. "You have wounded me in my tenderest feelings; you have destroyed my faith in women. I shall never be the same man again. I hope that you will never find out what a terrible mistake you've made."

Mrs. Bowman made a noise half-way between a sniff and a sob; Mr. Tucker's sniff was unmistakable.

"I will return your presents to-morrow," said Mr. Clark, rising. "Good-by, forever!"

He paused at the door, but Mrs. Bowman did not

look up. A second later the front door closed and she heard him walk rapidly away.

For some time after his departure she preserved a silence which Mr. Tucker endeavored in vain to break. He took a chair by her side, and at the third attempt managed to gain possession of her hand.

" I deserved all he said," she cried, at last. " Poor fellow, I hope he will do nothing desperate."

" No, no," said Mr. Tucker, soothingly.

" His eyes were quite wild," continued the widow. " If anything happens to him I shall never forgive myself. I have spoilt his life."

Mr. Tucker pressed her hand and spoke of the well-known refining influence a hopeless passion for a good woman had on a man. He cited his own case as an example.

" Disappointment spoilt my life so far as worldly success goes," he said, softly, " but no doubt the discipline was good for me."

Mrs. Bowman smiled faintly, and began to be a little comforted. Conversation shifted from the future of Mr. Clark to the past of Mr. Tucker; the widow's curiosity as to the extent of the latter's worldly success remaining unanswered by reason of Mr. Tucker's sudden remembrance of a bear-fight.

Their future was discussed after supper, and the advisability of leaving Trimington considered at some length. The towns and villages of England were at their disposal; Mr. Tucker's business, it appeared, being independent of place. He drew a picture of life in a bungalow with modern improvements at some seaside town, and, the cloth having been removed, took out his pocket-book and, extracting an old envelope, drew plans on the back.

It was a delightful pastime and made Mrs. Bowman feel that she was twenty and beginning life again. She toyed with the pocket-book and complimented Mr. Tucker on his skill as a draughtsman. A letter or two fell out and she replaced them. Then a small newspaper cutting, which had fluttered out with them, met her eye.

"A little veranda with roses climbing up it," murmured Mr. Tucker, still drawing, "and a couple of——"

His pencil was arrested by an odd, gasping noise from the window. He looked up and saw her sitting stiffly in her chair. Her face seemed to have swollen and to be colored in patches; her eyes were round and amazed.

"Aren't you well?" he inquired, rising in disorder.

Mrs. Bowman opened her lips, but no sound came from them. Then she gave a long, shivering sigh.

A Love-Knot

"Heat of the room too much for you?" inquired the other, anxiously.

Mrs. Bowman took another long, shivering breath. Still incapable of speech, she took the slip of paper in her trembling fingers and an involuntary exclamation of dismay broke from Mr. Tucker. She dabbed fiercely at her burning eyes with her handkerchief and read it again.

"TUCKER.—*If this should meet the eye of Charles Tucker, who knew Amelia Wyborn twenty-five years ago, he will hear of something greatly to his advantage by communicating with N. C., Royal Hotel, Northtown.*"

Mrs. Bowman found speech at last. "N. C.—Nathaniel Clark," she said, in broken tones. "So that is where he went last month. Oh, what a fool I've been! Oh, what a simple fool!"

Mr. Tucker gave a deprecatory cough. "I—I had forgotten it was there," he said, nervously.

"Yes," breathed the widow, "I can quite believe that."

"I was going to show you later on," declared the other, regarding her carefully. "I was, really. I couldn't bear the idea of keeping a secret from you long."

A Love-Knot

"'I had forgotten it was there,' he said, nervously."

A Love-Knot

Mrs. Bowman smiled—a terrible smile. "The audacity of the man," she broke out, "to stand there and lecture me on my behavior. To talk about his spoilt life, and all the time——"

She got up and walked about the room, angrily brushing aside the proffered attentions of Mr. Tucker.

"Laughing-stock of Trimington, is he?" she stormed. "He shall be more than that before I have done with him. The wickedness of the man; the artfulness!"

"That's what I thought," said Mr. Tucker, shaking his head. "I said to him——"

"You're as bad," said the widow, turning on him fiercely. "All the time you two men were talking at each other you were laughing in your sleeves at me. And I sat there like a child taking it all in. I've no doubt you met every night and arranged what you were to do next day."

Mr. Tucker's lips twitched. "I would do more than that to win you, Amelia," he said, humbly.

"You'll have to," was the grim reply. "Now I want to hear all about this from the beginning. And don't keep anything from me, or it'll be the worse for you."

She sat down again and motioned him to proceed.

A Love-Knot

"When I saw the advertisement in the *North-town Chronicle*," began Mr. Tucker, in husky voice, "I danced with——"

"Never mind about that," interrupted the widow, dryly.

"I went to the hotel and saw Mr. Clark," resumed Mr. Tucker, somewhat crestfallen. "When I heard that you were a widow, all the old times came back to me again. The years fell from me like a mantle. Once again I saw myself walking with you over the footpath to Cooper's farm; once again I felt your hand in mine. Your voice sounded in my ears——"

"You saw Mr. Clark," the widow reminded him.

"He had heard all about our early love from you," said Mr. Tucker, "and as a last desperate chance for freedom he had come down to try and hunt me up, and induce me to take you off his hands."

Mrs. Bowman uttered a smothered exclamation.

"He tempted me for two days," said Mr. Tucker, gravely. "The temptation was too great and I fell. Besides that, I wanted to rescue you from the clutches of such a man."

"Why didn't he tell me himself?" inquired the widow.

"Just what I asked him," said the other, "but he

said that you were much too fond of him to give him up. He is not worthy of you, Amelia; he is fickle. He has got his eye on another lady."

" WHAT? " said the widow, with sudden loudness.

Mr. Tucker nodded mournfully. " Miss Hackbutt," he said, slowly. " I saw her the other day, and what he can see in her I can't think."

" Miss Hackbutt? " repeated the widow in a smothered voice. " Miss——" She got up and began to pace the room again.

" He must be blind," said Mr. Tucker, positively.

Mrs. Bowman stopped suddenly and stood regarding him. There was a light in her eye which made him feel anything but comfortable. He was glad when she transferred her gaze to the clock. She looked at it so long that he murmured something about going.

" Good-by," she said.

Mr. Tucker began to repeat his excuses, but she interrupted him. " Not now," she said, decidedly. " I'm tired. Good-night."

Mr. Tucker pressed her hand. " Good-night," he said, tenderly. " I am afraid the excitement has been too much for you. May I come round at the usual time to-morrow? "

" Yes," said the widow.

She took the advertisement from the table and,

A Love-Knot

folding it carefully, placed it in her purse. Mr. Tucker withdrew as she looked up.

He walked back to the " George " deep in thought, and over a couple of pipes in bed thought over the events of the evening. He fell asleep at last and dreamed that he and Miss Hackbutt were being united in the bonds of holy matrimony by the Rev. Nathaniel Clark.

The vague misgivings of the previous night disappeared in the morning sunshine. He shaved carefully and spent some time in the selection of a tie. Over an excellent breakfast he arranged further explanations and excuses for the appeasement of Mrs. Bowman.

He was still engaged on the task when he started to call on her. Half-way to the house he arrived at the conclusion that he was looking too cheerful. His face took on an expression of deep seriousness, only to give way the next moment to one of the blankest amazement. In front of him, and approaching with faltering steps, was Mr. Clark, and leaning trustfully on his arm the comfortable figure of Mrs. Bowman. Her brow was unruffled and her lips smiling.

" Beautiful morning," she said, pleasantly, as they met.

" Lovely ! " murmured the wondering Mr.

Tucker, trying, but in vain, to catch the eye of Mr. Clark.

"I have been paying an early visit," said the widow, still smiling. "I surprised you, didn't I, Nathaniel?"

"You did," said Mr. Clark, in an unearthly voice.

"We got talking about last night," continued the widow, "and Nathaniel started pleading with me to give him another chance. I suppose that I am soft-hearted, but he was so miserable—— You were never so miserable in your life before, were you, Nathaniel?"

"Never," said Mr. Clark, in the same strange voice.

"He was so wretched that at last I gave way," said Mrs. Bowman, with a simper. "Poor fellow, it was such a shock to him that he hasn't got back his cheerfulness yet."

Mr. Tucker said, "Indeed!"

"He'll be all right soon," said Mrs. Bowman, in confidential tones. "We are on the way to put our banns up, and once that is done he will feel safe. You are not really afraid of losing me again, are you, Nathaniel?"

Mr. Clark shook his head, and, meeting the eye of Mr. Tucker in the process, favored him with a glance of such utter venom that the latter was almost startled.

"Good-by, Mr. Tucker," said the widow, holding out her hand. "Nathaniel did think of inviting you to come to my wedding, but perhaps it is best not. However, if I alter my mind, I will get him to advertise for you again. Good-by."

She placed her arm in Mr. Clark's again, and led him slowly away. Mr. Tucker stood watching them for some time, and then, with a glance in the direction of the "George," where he had left a very small portmanteau, he did a hasty sum in comparative values and made his way to the railway-station.

HER UNCLE

Her Uncle

MR. WRAGG sat in a high-backed Windsor chair at the door of his house, smoking. Before him the road descended steeply to the harbor, a small blue patch of which was visible from his door. Children over five were at school; children under that age, and suspiciously large for their years, played about in careless disregard of the remarks which Mr. Wragg occasionally launched at them. Twice a ball had whizzed past him; and a small but select party, with a tip-cat of huge dimensions and awesome points, played just out of reach. Mr. Wragg, snapping his eyes nervously, threatened in vain.

"Morning, old crusty-patch," said a cheerful voice at his elbow.

Mr. Wragg glanced up at the young fisherman towering above him, and eyed him disdainfully.

"Why don't you leave 'em alone?" inquired the young man. "Be cheerful and smile at 'em. You'd soon be able to smile with a little practice."

Her Uncle

"You mind your business, George Gale, and I'll mind mine," said Mr. Wragg, fiercely; " I've 'ad enough of your impudence, and I'm not going to have any more. And don't lean up agin my house, 'cos I won't 'ave it."

Mr. Gale laughed. " Got out o' bed the wrong side again, haven't you? " he inquired. " Why don't you put that side up against the wall? "

Mr. Wragg puffed on in silence and became absorbed in a fishing-boat gliding past at the bottom of the hill.

" I hear you've got a niece coming to live with you? " pursued the young man.

Mr. Wragg smoked on.

" Poor thing! " said the other, with a sigh. " Does she take after you—in looks, I mean? "

" If I was twenty years younger nor what I am," said Mr. Wragg, sententiously, " I'd give you a hiding, George Gale."

" It's what I want," agreed Mr. Gale, placidly. " Well, so long, Mr. Wragg. I can't stand talking to you all day."

He was about to move off, after pretending to pinch the ear of the infuriated Mr. Wragg, when he noticed a station-fly, with a big trunk on the box-seat, crawling slowly up the hill towards them.

" Good riddance," said Mr. Wragg, suggestively.

Her Uncle

The other paid no heed. The vehicle came nearer, and a girl, who plainly owed none of her looks to Mr. Wragg's side of the family, came into view behind the trunk. She waved her hand, and Mr. Wragg, removing his pipe from his mouth, waved it in return. Mr. Gale edged away about eighteen inches, and, with an air of assumed carelessness, gazed idly about him.

He saluted the driver as the fly stopped and gazed hard at the apparition that descended. Then he caught his breath as the girl, approaching her uncle, kissed him affectionately. Mr. Wragg, looking up fiercely at Mr. Gale, was surprised at the expression on that gentleman's face.

" Isn't it lovely here? " said the girl, looking about her; " and isn't the air nice? "

She followed Mr. Wragg inside, and the driver, a small man and elderly, began tugging at the huge trunk. Mr. Gale's moment had arrived.

" Stand away, Joe," he said, stepping forward. " I'll take that in for you."

He hoisted the trunk on his shoulders, and, rather glad of his lowered face, advanced slowly into the house. Uncle and niece had just vanished at the head of the stairs, and Mr. Gale, after a moment's hesitation, followed.

" In 'ere," said Mr. Wragg, throwing open a door.

Her Uncle

"Halloa! What are you doing in my house? Put it down. Put it down at once; d'ye hear?"

Mr. Gale caught the girl's surprised glance and, somewhat flustered, swung round so suddenly that the corner of the trunk took the gesticulating Mr. Wragg by the side of the head and bumped it against the wall. Deaf to his outcries, Mr. Gale entered the room and placed the box on the floor.

"Where shall I put it?" he inquired of the girl, respectfully.

"You go out of my house," stormed Mr. Wragg, entering with his hand to his head. "Go on. Out you go."

The young man surveyed him with solicitude. "I'm very sorry if I hurt you, Mr. Wragg——" he began.

"Out you go," repeated the other.

"It was a pure accident," pleaded Mr. Gale.

"And don't you set foot in my 'ouse agin," said the vengeful Mr. Wragg. "You made yourself officious bringing that box in a-purpose to give me a clump o' the side of the head with it."

Mr. Gale denied the charge so eagerly, and withal so politely, that the elder man regarded him in amazement. Then his glance fell on his niece, and he smiled with sudden malice as Mr. Gale slowly and humbly descended the stairs.

Her Uncle

"The corner of the trunk took the gesticulating Mr. Wragg by the side of the head."

"One o' the worst chaps about here, my dear," he said, loudly. "Mate o' one o' the fishing-boats, and as impudent as they make 'em. Many's the time I've clouted his head for 'im."

The girl regarded his small figure with surprised respect.

"When he was a boy, I mean," continued Mr. Wragg. "Now, there's your room, and when you've put things to rights, come down and I'll show you over the house."

He glanced at his niece several times during the day, trying hard to trace a likeness, first to his dead sister and then to himself. Several times he scrutinized himself in the small glass on the mantelpiece, but in vain. Even when he twisted his thin beard in his hand and tried to ignore his mustache, the likeness still eluded him.

His opinion of Miss Miller's looks was more than shared by the young men of Waterside. It was a busy youth who could not spare five minutes to chat with an uncle so fortunate, and in less than a couple of weeks Mr. Wragg was astonished at his popularity, and the deference accorded to his opinions.

The most humble of them all was Mr. Gale, and, with a pertinacity which was almost proof against insult, he strove to force his company upon the indignant Mr. Wragg. Debarred from that, he took to

Her Uncle

haunting the road, on one occasion passing the house no fewer than fifty-seven times in one afternoon. His infatuation was plain to be seen of all men. Wise men closed their eyes to it; others had theirs closed for them, Mr. Gale being naturally incensed to think that there was anything in his behavior that attracted attention.

His father was at sea, and, to the dismay of the old woman who kept house for him, he began to neglect his food. A melancholy but not unpleasing idea that he was slowly fading occurred to him when he found that he could eat only two herrings for breakfast instead of four. His particular friend, Joe Harris, to whom he confided the fact, remonstrated hotly.

"There's plenty of other girls," he suggested.

"Not like her," said Mr. Gale.

"You're getting to be a by-word in the place," complained his friend.

Mr. Gale flushed. "I'd do more than that for her sake," he said, softly.

"It ain't the way," said Mr. Harris, impatiently. "Girls like a man o' spirit; not a chap who hangs about without speaking, and looks as though he has been caught stealing the cat's milk. Why don't you go round and see her one afternoon when old Wragg is out?"

Her Uncle

Mr. Gale shivered. " I dursen't," he confessed.

Mr. Harris pondered. " She was going to be a hospital nurse afore she came down here," he said, slowly. " P'r'aps if you was to break your leg or something she'd come and nurse you. She's wonderful fond of it, I understand."

" But then, you see, I haven't broken it," said the other, impatiently.

" You've got a bicycle," said Mr. Harris. " You —wait a minute——" he half-closed his eyes and waved aside a remark of his friend's. " Suppose you 'ad an accident and fell off it, just in front of the house? "

" I never fall off," said Mr. Gale, simply.

" Old Wragg is out, and me and Charlie Brown carry you into the house," continued Mr. Harris, closing his eyes entirely. " When you come to your senses, she's bending over you and crying."

He opened his eyes suddenly and then, closing one, gazed hard at the bewildered Gale. " To-morrow afternoon at two," he said, briskly, " me and Charlie'll be there waiting."

" Suppose old Wragg ain't out? " objected Mr. Gale, after ten minutes' explanation.

" He's at the ' Lobster Pot ' five days out of six at that time," was the reply; " if he ain't there to-morrow, it can't be helped."

Her Uncle

Mr. Gale spent the evening practising falls in a quiet lane, and by the time night came had attained to such proficiency that on the way home he fell off without intending it. It seemed an easier thing than he had imagined, and next day at two o'clock punctually he put his lessons into practice.

By a slight error in judgment his head came into contact with Mr. Wragg's doorstep, and, half-stunned, he was about to rise, when Mr. Harris rushed up and forced him down again. Mr. Brown, who was also in attendance, helped to restore his faculties by a well-placed kick.

" He's lost his senses," said Mr. Harris, looking up at Miss Miller, as she came to the door.

" You could ha' heard him fall arf a mile away," added Mr. Brown.

Miss Miller stooped and examined the victim carefully. There was a nasty cut on the side of his head, and a general limpness of body which was alarming. She went indoors for some water, and by the time she returned the enterprising Mr. Harris had got the patient in the passage.

" I'm afraid he's going," he said, in answer to the girl's glance.

" Run for the doctor," she said, hastily. " Quick ! "

" We don't like to leave 'im, miss," said Mr.

Her Uncle

Harris, tenderly. " I s'pose it would be too much to ask you to go? "

Miss Miller, with a parting glance at the prostrate man, departed at once.

" What did you do that for? " demanded Mr. Gale, sitting up. " I don't want the doctor; he'll spoil everything. Why didn't you go away and leave us? "

" I sent 'er for the doctor," said Mr. Harris, slowly. " I sent 'er for the doctor so as we can get you to bed afore she comes back."

" *Bed?* " exclaimed Mr. Gale.

" Up you go," said Mr. Harris, briefly. " We'll tell *her* we carried you up. Now, don't waste time."

Pushed by his friends, and stopping to expostulate at every step, Mr. Gale was thrust at last into Mr. Wragg's bedroom.

" Off with your clothes," said the leading spirit. " What's the matter with you, Charlie Brown? "

" Don't mind me; I'll be all right in a minute," said that gentleman, wiping his eyes. " I'm thinking of old Wragg."

Before Mr. Gale had made up his mind his coat and waistcoat were off, and Mr. Brown was at work on his boots. In five minutes' time he was tucked up in Mr. Wragg's bed; his clothes were in a neat little pile on a chair, and Messrs. Har-

Her Uncle

" ' What did you do that for ?' demanded Mr. Gale, sitting up."

ris and Brown were indulging in a congratulatory double-shuffle by the window.

"Don't come to your senses yet awhile," said the former; "and when you do, tell the doctor you can't move your limbs."

"If they try to pull you out o' bed," said Mr. Brown, "scream as though you're being killed. *H'sh!* Here they are."

Voices sounded below; Miss Miller and the doctor had met at the door with Mr. Wragg, and a violent outburst on that gentleman's part died away as he saw that the intruders had disappeared. He was still grumbling when Mr. Harris, putting his head over the balusters, asked him to make a little less noise.

Mr. Wragg came upstairs in three bounds, and his mien was so terrible that Messrs. Harris and Brown huddled together for protection. Then his gaze fell on the bed and he strove in vain for speech.

"We done it for the best," faltered Mr. Harris.

Mr. Wragg made a gurgling noise in his throat, and, as the doctor entered the room, pointed with a trembling finger at the bed. The other two gentlemen edged toward the door.

"Take him away; take him away at once," vociferated Mr. Wragg.

Her Uncle

The doctor motioned him to silence, and Joe Harris and Mr. Brown held their breaths nervously as he made an examination. For ten minutes he prodded and puzzled over the insensible form in the bed; then he turned to the couple at the door.

"How did it happen?" he inquired.

Mr. Harris told him. He also added that he thought it was best to put him to bed at once before he came round.

"Quite right," said the doctor, nodding. "It's a very serious case."

"Well, I can't 'ave him 'ere," broke in Mr. Wragg.

"It won't be for long," said the doctor, shaking his head.

"I can't 'ave him 'ere at all, and, what's more, I won't. Let him go to his own bed," said Mr. Wragg, quivering with excitement.

"He is not to be moved," said the doctor, decidedly. "If he comes to his senses and gets out of bed you must coax him back again."

"Coax?" stuttered Mr. Wragg. "Coax? What's he got to do with me? This house isn't a 'orsepittle. Put his clothes on and take 'im away."

"Do nothing of the kind," was the stern reply. "In fact, his clothes had better be taken out of the room, in case he comes round and tries to dress."

Mr. Harris skipped across to the clothes and tucked them gleefully under his arm; Mr. Brown secured the boots.

"When he will come out of this stupor I can't say," continued the doctor. "Keep him perfectly quiet and don't let him see a soul."

"Look 'ere——" began Mr. Wragg, in a broken voice.

"As to diet—water," said the doctor, looking round.

"Water?" said Miss Miller, who had come quietly into the room.

"Water," repeated the doctor; "as much as he likes to take, of course. Let me see: to-day is Tuesday. I'll look in on Friday, or Saturday at latest; but till then he must have nothing but clear cold water."

Mr. Harris shot a horrified glance at the bed, which happened just then to creak. "But s'pose he asks for food, sir?" he said, respectfully.

"He mustn't have it," said the other, sharply. "If he is very insistent," he added, turning to the sullen Mr. Wragg, "tell him that he has just had food. He won't know any better, and he will be quite satisfied."

Her Uncle

He motioned them out of the room, and then, lowering the blinds, followed downstairs on tiptoe. A murmur of voices, followed by the closing of the front door, sounded from below; and Mr. Gale, getting cautiously out of bed, saw Messrs. Harris and Brown walk up the street talking earnestly. He stole back on tiptoe to the door, and strove in vain to catch the purport of the low-voiced discussion below. Mr. Wragg's voice was raised, but indistinct. Then he fancied that he heard a laugh.

He waited until the door closed behind the doctor, and then went back to bed, to try and think out a situation which was fast becoming mysterious.

He lay in the darkened room until a cheerful clatter of crockery below heralded the approach of tea-time. He heard Miss Miller call her uncle in from the garden, and with some satisfaction heard her pleasant voice engaged in brisk talk. At intervals Mr. Wragg laughed loud and long.

Tea was cleared away, and the long evening dragged along in silence. Uncle and niece were apparently sitting in the garden, but they came in to supper, and later on the fumes of Mr. Wragg's pipe pervaded the house. At ten o'clock he heard footsteps ascending the stairs, and through half-

closed eyes saw Mr. Wragg enter the bedroom with
a candle.

" Time the pore feller had 'is water," he said to
his niece, who remained outside.

" Unless he is still insensible," was the reply.

Mr. Gale, who was feeling both thirsty and
hungry, slowly opened his eyes, and fixed them in
a vacant stare on Mr. Wragg.

" Where am I ? " he inquired, in a faint voice.

" Buckingham Pallis," replied Mr. Wragg,
promptly.

Mr. Gale ground his teeth. " How did I come
here ? " he said, at last.

" The fairies brought you," said Mr. Wragg.

The young man rubbed his eyes and blinked at
the candle. " I seem to remember falling," he
said, slowly; " has anything happened? "

" One o' the fairies dropped you," said Mr.
Wragg, with great readiness; " fortunately, you fell
on your head."

A sound suspiciously like a giggle came from the
landing and fell heavily on Gale's ears. He closed
his eyes and tried to think.

" How did I get into your bedroom, Mr.
Wragg " he inquired, after a long pause.

" Light-'eaded," confided Mr. Wragg to the
landing, and significantly tapping his forehead.

Her Uncle

"This ain't my bedroom," he said, turning to the invalid. "It's the King's. His Majesty gave up 'is bed at once, direckly he 'eard you was 'urt."

"And he's going to sleep on three chairs in the front parlor—if he can," said a low voice from the landing.

The humor faded from Mr. Wragg's face and was succeeded by an expression of great sourness. "Where is the pore feller's supper?" he inquired. "I don't suppose he can eat anything, but he might try."

He went to the door and a low-voiced colloquy ensued. The rival merits of cold chicken versus steak-pie as an invalid diet were discussed at some length. Finally the voice of Miss Miller insisted on chicken, and a glass of port-wine.

"I'll tell 'im it's chicken and port-wine then," said Mr. Wragg, reappearing with a bedroom jug and a tumbler, which he placed on a small table by the bedside.

"Don't let him eat too much, mind," said the voice from the landing, anxiously.

Mr. Wragg said that he would be careful, and addressing Mr. Gale implored him not to overeat himself. The young man stared at him offensively, and, pretty certain now of the true state of affairs, thought only of escape.

Her Uncle

"I feel better," he said, slowly. "I think I will go home."

"Yes, yes," said the other, soothingly.

"If you will fetch my clothes," continued Mr. Gale, "I will go now."

"*Clothes!*" said Mr. Wragg, in an astonished voice. "Why, you didn't 'ave any."

Mr. Gale sat up suddenly in bed and shook his fist at him. "Look here——" he began, in a choking voice.

"The fairies brought you as you was," continued Mr. Wragg, grinning furiously; "and of all the perfect picturs——"

A series of gasping sobs sounded from the landing, the stairs creaked, and a door slammed violently below. In spite of this precaution the sounds of a maiden in dire distress were distinctly audible.

. "You give me my clothes," shouted the now furious Mr. Gale, springing out of bed.

Mr. Wragg drew back. "I'll go and fetch 'em," he said, hastily.

He ran lightly downstairs, and the young man, sitting on the edge of the bed, waited. Ten minutes passed, and he heard Mr. Wragg returning, followed by his niece. He slipped back into bed again.

"It's a pore brain again," he heard, in the

Her Uncle

unctuous tones which Mr. Wragg appeared to keep for this emergency. " It's clothes he wants now; by and by I suppose it'll be something else. Well, the doctor said we'd got to humor him."

" Poor fellow! " sighed Miss Miller, with a break in her voice.

" See 'ow his face'll light up when he sees them," said her uncle.

He pushed the door open, and after surveying the patient with a benevolent smile triumphantly held up a collar and tie for his inspection and threw them on the bed. Then he disappeared hastily and, closing the door, turned the key in the lock.

" If you want any more chicken or anything," he cried through the door, " ring the bell."

The horrified prisoner heard them pass downstairs again, and, after a glass of water, sat down by the window and tried to think. He got up and tried the door, but it opened inwards, and after a severe onslaught the handle came off in his hand. Tired out at last he went to bed again, and slept fitfully until morning.

Mr. Wragg visited him again after breakfast, but with great foresight only put his head in at the door, while Miss Miller remained outside in case of need. In these circumstances Mr. Gale

met his anxious inquiries with a sullen silence, and
the other, tired at last of baiting him, turned to go.

"I'll be back soon," he said, with a grin. "I'm
just going out to tell folks 'ow you're getting on.
There's a lot of 'em anxious."

He was as good as his word, and Mr. Gale,
peeping from the window, raged helplessly as little
knots of neighbors stood smiling up at the house.
Unable to endure it any longer he returned to bed,
resolving to wait until night came, and then drop
from the window and run home in a blanket.

The smell of dinner was almost painful, but he
made no sign. Mr. Wragg in high good humor
smoked a pipe after his meal, and then went out
again. The house was silent except for the occasional movements of the girl below. Then there
was a sudden tap at his door.

"Well?" said Mr. Gale.

The door opened and, hardly able to believe
his eyes, he saw his clothes thrown into the room.
Hunger was forgotten, and he almost smiled as he
hastily dressed himself.

The smile vanished as he thought of the people
in the streets, and in a thoughtful fashion he made
his way slowly downstairs. The bright face of
Miss Miller appeared at the parlor door.

"Better?" she smiled.

Her Uncle

Mr. Gale reddened and, drawing himself up stiffly, made no reply.

"That's polite," said the girl, indignantly. "After giving you your clothes, too. What do you think my uncle will say to me? He was going to keep you here till Friday."

Mr. Gale muttered an apology. "I've made a fool of myself," he added.

Miss Miller nodded cheerfully. "Are you hungry?" she inquired.

The other drew himself up again.

"Because there is some nice cold beef left," said the girl, glancing into the room.

Mr. Gale started and, hardly able to believe in his good fortune, followed her inside. In a very short time the cold beef was a thing of the past, and the young man, toying with his beer-glass, sat listening to a lecture on his behavior couched in the severest terms his hostess could devise.

"You'll be the laughing-stock of the place," she concluded.

"I shall go away," he said, gloomily.

"I shouldn't do that," said the girl, with a judicial air; "live it down."

"I shall go away," repeated Mr. Gale, decidedly. "I shall ship for a deep-sea voyage."

Miss Miller sighed. "It's too bad," she said,

Her Uncle

slowly; "perhaps you wouldn't look so foolish if——"

"If what?" inquired the other, after a long pause.

"If," said Miss Miller, looking down, "if—if——"

Mr. Gale started and trembled violently, as a wild idea, born of her blushes, occurred to him.

"If," he said, in quivering tones, "if—if——"

"Go on," said the girl, softly. "Why, I got as far as that: and you are a man."

Mr. Gale's voice became almost inaudible. "If we got married, do you mean?" he said, at last.

"Married!" exclaimed Miss Miller, starting back a full two inches. "Good gracious! the man *is* mad after all."

The bitter and loudly expressed opinion of Mr. Wragg when he returned an hour later was that they were both mad.

THE DREAMER

The Dreamer

DREAMS and warnings are things I don't believe in, said the night watchman. The only dream I ever 'ad that come anything like true was once when I dreamt I came in for a fortune, and next morning I found half a crown in the street, which I sold to a man for fourpence. And once, two days arter my missis 'ad dreamt she 'ad spilt a cup of tea down the front of 'er Sunday dress, she spoilt a pot o' paint of mine by sitting in it.

The only other dream I know of that come true happened to the cook of a bark I was aboard of once, called the *Southern Belle*. He was a silly, pasty-faced sort o' chap, always giving hisself airs about eddication to sailormen who didn't believe in it, and one night, when we was homeward-bound from Sydney, he suddenly sat up in 'is bunk and laughed so loud that he woke us all up.

" Wot's wrong, cookie? " ses one o' the chaps.

The Dreamer

" I was dreaming," ses the cook, " such a funny dream. I dreamt old Bill Foster fell out o' the foretop and broke 'is leg."

" Well, wot is there to laugh at in that? " ses old Bill, very sharp.

" It was funny in my dream," ses the cook. " You looked so comic with your leg doubled up under you, you can't think. It would ha' made a cat laugh."

Bill Foster said he'd make 'im laugh the other side of his face if he wasn't careful, and then we went off to sleep agin and forgot all about it.

If you'll believe me, on'y three days arterwards pore Bill did fall out o' the foretop and break his leg. He was surprised, but I never see a man so surprised as the cook was. His eyes was nearly starting out of 'is head, but by the time the other chaps 'ad picked Bill up and asked 'im whether he was hurt, cook 'ad pulled 'imself together agin and was giving himself such airs it was perfectly sickening.

" My dreams always come true," he ses. " It's a kind o' second sight with me. It's a gift, and, being tender-'arted, it worries me terrible sometimes."

He was going on like that, taking credit for a pure accident, when the second officer came up and

The Dreamer

told 'em to carry Bill below. He was in agony, of course, but he kept 'is presence of mind, and as they passed the cook he gave 'im such a clip on the side of the 'ead as nearly broke it.

" That's for dreaming about me," he ses.

The skipper and the fust officer and most of the hands set 'is leg between them, and arter the skipper 'ad made him wot he called comfortable, but wot Bill called something that I won't soil my ears by repeating, the officers went off and the cook came and sat down by the side o' Bill and talked about his gift.

" I don't talk about it as a rule," he ses, " 'cos it frightens people."

" It's a wonderful gift, cookie," ses Charlie Epps.

All of 'em thought the same, not knowing wot a fust-class liar the cook was, and he sat there and lied to 'em till he couldn't 'ardly speak, he was so 'oarse.

" My grandmother was a gypsy," he ses, " and it's in the family. Things that are going to 'appen to people I know come to me in dreams, same as pore Bill's did. It's curious to me sometimes when I look round at you chaps, seeing you going about 'appy and comfortable, and knowing all the time 'orrible things that is going to 'appen to you. Sometimes it gives me the fair shivers."

" Horrible things to us, slushy? " ses Charlie, staring.

" Yes," ses the cook, nodding. " I never was on a ship afore with such a lot of unfortunit men aboard. Never. There's two pore fellers wot'll be dead corpses inside o' six months, sitting 'ere laughing and talking as if they was going to live to ninety. Thank your stars you don't 'ave such dreams."

" Who—who are the two, cookie? " ses Charlie, arter a bit.

" Never mind, Charlie," ses the cook, in a sad voice; " it would do no good if I was to tell you. Nothing can alter it."

" Give us a hint," ses Charlie.

" Well, I'll tell you this much," ses the cook, arter sitting with his 'ead in his 'ands, thinking; " one of 'em is nearly the ugliest man in the fo'c's'le and the other ain't."

O' course, that didn't 'elp 'em much, but it caused a lot of argufying, and the ugliest man aboard, instead o' being grateful, behaved more like a wild beast than a Christian when it was pointed out to him that he was safe.

Arter that dream about Bill, there was no keep-

The Dreamer

ing the cook in his place. He 'ad dreams pretty near every night, and talked little bits of 'em in his sleep. Little bits that you couldn't make head nor tail of, and when we asked 'im next morning he'd always shake his 'ead and say, " Never mind." Sometimes he'd mention a chap's name in 'is sleep and make 'im nervous for days.

It was an unlucy v'y'ge that, for some of 'em. About a week arter pore Bill's accident Ted Jones started playing catch-ball with another chap and a empty beer-bottle, and about the fifth chuck Ted caught it with his face. We thought 'e was killed at fust—he made such a noise; but they got 'im down below, and, arter they 'ad picked out as much broken glass as Ted would let 'em, the second officer did 'im up in sticking-plaster and told 'im to keep quiet for an hour or two.

Ted was very proud of 'is looks, and the way he went on was alarming. Fust of all he found fault with the chap 'e was playing with, and then he turned on the cook.

" It's a pity you didn't see *that* in a dream," he ses, tryin' to sneer, on'y the sticking-plaster was too strong for 'im.

" But I did see it," ses the cook, drawin' 'imself up.

" *Wot?* " ses Ted, starting.

The Dreamer

"I dreamt it night afore last, just exactly as it 'appened," ses the cook, in a offhand way.

"Why didn't you tell me, then?" ses Ted choking.

"It 'ud ha' been no good," ses the cook, smiling and shaking his 'ead. "Wot I see must 'appen. I on'y see the future, and that must be."

"But you stood there watching me chucking the bottle about," ses Ted, getting out of 'is bunk. "Why didn't you stop me?"

"You don't understand," ses the cook. "If you'd 'ad more eddication——"

He didn't 'ave time to say any more afore Ted was on him, and cookie, being no fighter, 'ad to cook with one eye for the next two or three days. He kept quiet about 'is dreams for some time arter that, but it was no good, because George Hall, wot was a firm believer, gave 'im a licking for not warning 'im of a sprained ankle he got skylarking, and Bob Law took it out of 'im for not telling 'im that he was going to lose 'is suit of shore-going togs at cards.

The only chap that seemed to show any good feeling for the cook was a young feller named Joseph Meek, a steady young chap wot was goin' to be married to old Bill Foster's niece as soon as we got 'ome. Nobody else knew it, but he told

The Dreamer

" ' Why didn't you tell me, then ? ' ses Ted."

The Dreamer

the cook all about it on the quiet. He said she was too good for 'im, but, do all he could, he couldn't get her to see it.

" My feelings 'ave changed," he ses.

" P'r'aps they'll change agin," ses the cook, trying to comfort 'im.

Joseph shook his 'ead. " No, I've made up my mind," he ses, very slow. " I'm young yet, and, besides, I can't afford it; but 'ow to get out of it I don't know. Couldn't you 'ave a dream agin it for me? "

" Wot d'ye mean? " ses the cook, firing up. " Do you think I make my dreams up? "

" No, no; cert'inly not," ses Joseph, patting 'im on the shoulder; " but couldn't you do it just for once? 'Ave a dream that me and Emily are killed a few days arter the wedding. Don't say in wot way, 'cos she might think we could avoid it; just dream we are killed. Bill's always been a superstitious man, and since you dreamt about his leg he'd believe anything; and he's that fond of Emily I believe he'd 'ave the wedding put off, at any rate—if I put him up to it."

It took 'im three days and a silver watch-chain to persuade the cook, but he did at last; and one arternoon, when old Bill, who was getting on fust-class, was resting 'is leg in 'is bunk,

The Dreamer

the cook went below and turned in for a quiet sleep.

For ten minutes he was as peaceful as a lamb, and old Bill, who 'ad been laying in 'is bunk with an eye open watching 'im, was just dropping off 'imself, when the cook began to talk in 'is sleep, and the very fust words made Bill sit up as though something 'ad bit 'im.

"There they go," ses the cook, "Emily Foster and Joseph Meek—and there's old Bill, good old Bill, going to give the bride away. How 'appy they all look, especially Joseph!"

Old Bill put his 'and to his ear and leaned out of his bunk.

"There they go," ses the cook agin; "but wot is that 'orrible black thing with claws that's 'anging over Bill?"

Pore Bill nearly fell out of 'is bunk, but he saved 'imself at the last moment and lay there as pale as death, listening.

"It must be meant for Bill," ses the cook. "Well, pore Bill; he won't know of it, that's one thing. Let's 'ope it'll be sudden."

He lay quiet for some time and then he began again.

"No," he ses, "it isn't Bill; it's Joseph and Emily, stark and stiff, and they've on'y been married a week. 'Ow awful they look! Pore things. Oh! oh! o-oh!"

He woke up with a shiver and began to groan and then 'e sat up in his bunk and saw old Bill leaning out and staring at 'im.

"You've been dreaming, cook," ses Bill, in a trembling voice.

"'Ave I?" ses the cook. "How do you know?"

"About me and my niece," ses Bill; "you was talking in your sleep."

"You oughtn't to 'ave listened," ses the cook, getting out of 'is bunk and going over to 'im. "I 'ope you didn't 'ear all I dreamt. 'Ow much did you hear?"

Bill told 'im, and the cook sat there, shaking his 'ead. "Thank goodness, you didn't 'ear the worst of it," he ses.

"*Worst!*" ses Bill. "Wot, was there any more of it?"

"Lot's more," ses the cook. "But promise me you won't tell Joseph, Bill. Let 'im be happy while he can; it would on'y make 'im miserable, and it wouldn't do any good."

"I don't know so much about that," ses Bill, thinking about the arguments some of them had 'ad with Ted about the bottle. "Was it arter they was married, cookie, that it 'appened? Are you sure?"

The Dreamer

"Certain sure. It was a week arter," ses the cook.

"Very well, then," ses Bill, slapping 'is bad leg by mistake; "if they didn't marry, it couldn't 'appen, could it?"

"Don't talk foolish," ses the cook; "they must marry. I saw it in my dream."

"Well, we'll see," ses Bill. "I'm going to 'ave a quiet talk with Joseph about it, and see wot he ses. I ain't a-going to 'ave my pore gal murdered just to please you and make your dreams come true."

He 'ad a quiet talk with Joseph, but Joseph wouldn't 'ear of it at fust. He said it was all the cook's nonsense, though 'e owned up that it was funny that the cook should know about the wedding and Emily's name, and at last he said that they would put it afore Emily and let her decide.

That was about the last dream the cook had that v'y'ge, although he told old Bill one day that he had 'ad the same dream about Joseph and Emily agin, so that he was quite certain they 'ad got to be married and killed. He wouldn't tell Bill 'ow they was to be killed, because 'e said it would make 'im an old man afore his time; but, of course, he 'ad to say that *if* they wasn't married the other part couldn't come true. He said that as he 'ad never told 'is dreams before—except in the case of Bill's leg—he couldn't say for certain that they couldn't be prevented by taking care, but p'r'aps, they could; and Bill pointed out to 'im wot a useful man he would be if he could dream and warn people in time.

By the time we got into the London river old Bill's leg was getting on fust-rate, and he got along splendid on a pair of crutches the carpenter 'ad made for him. Him and Joseph and the cook had 'ad a good many talks about the dream, and the old man 'ad invited the cook to come along 'ome with 'em, to be referred to when he told the tale.

" I shall take my opportunity," he ses, " and break it to 'er gentle like. When I speak to you, you chip in, and not afore. D'ye understand?"

We went into the East India Docks that v'y'ge, and got there early on a lovely summer's evening. Everybody was 'arf crazy at the idea o' going ashore agin, and working as cheerful and as willing as if they liked it. There was a few people standing on the pier-head as we went in, and among 'em several very nice-looking young wimmen.

" My eye, Joseph," ses the cook, who 'ad been staring hard at one of 'em, " there's a fine gal—lively, too. Look 'ere!"

He kissed 'is dirty paw—which is more than I

The Dreamer

"'I shall take my opportunity,' he ses, 'and break it to 'er gentle like.'"

should 'ave liked to 'ave done it if it 'ad been mine
—and waved it, and the gal turned round and
shook her 'ead at 'im.

"Here, that'll do," ses Joseph, very cross.
"That's my gal; that's my Emily."

"Eh?" says the cook. "Well, 'ow was I to
know? Besides, you're a-giving of her up."

Joseph didn't answer 'im. He was staring at
Emily, and the more he stared the better-looking
she seemed to grow. She really was an uncommon nice-looking gal, and more than the cook was
struck with her.

"Who's that chap standing alongside of her?"
ses the cook.

"It's one o' Bill's sister's lodgers," ses Joseph,
who was looking very bad-tempered. "I should
like to know wot right he 'as to come 'ere to welcome me 'ome. I don't want 'im."

"P'r'aps he's fond of 'er," ses the cook. "I
could be, very easy."

"I'll chuck 'im in the dock if he ain't careful,"
ses Joseph, turning red in the face.

He waved his 'and to Emily, who didn't 'appen
to be looking at the moment, but the lodger waved
back in a careless sort of way and then spoke to
Emily, and they both waved to old Bill who was
standing on his crutches further aft.

The Dreamer

By the time the ship was berthed and everything snug it was quite dark, and old Bill didn't know whether to take the cook 'ome with 'im and break the news that night, or wait a bit. He made up his mind at last to get it over and done with, and arter waiting till the cook 'ad cleaned 'imself they got a cab and drove off.

Bert Simmons, the lodger, 'ad to ride on the box, and Bill took up so much room with 'is bad leg that Emily found it more comfortable to sit on Joseph's knee; and by the time they got to the 'ouse he began to see wot a silly mistake he was making.

"Keep that dream o' yours to yourself till I make up my mind," he ses to the cook, while Bill and the cabman were calling each other names.

"Bill's going to speak fust," whispers the cook.

The lodger and Emily 'ad gone inside, and Joseph stood there, fidgeting, while the cabman asked Bill, as a friend, why he 'adn't paid two-pence more for his face, and Bill was wasting his time trying to think of something to say to 'urt the cabman's feelings. Then he took Bill by the arm as the cab drove off and told 'im not to say nothing about the dream, because he was going to risk it.

The Dreamer

"Stuff and nonsense," ses Bill. "I'm going to tell Emily. It's my dooty. Wot's the good o' being married if you're going to be killed?"

He stumped in on his crutches afore Joseph could say any more, and, arter letting his sister kiss 'im, went into the front room and sat down. There was cold beef and pickles on the table and two jugs o' beer, and arter just telling his sister 'ow he fell and broke 'is leg, they all sat down to supper.

Bert Simmons sat on one side of Emily and Joseph the other, and the cook couldn't 'elp feeling sorry for 'er, seeing as he did that sometimes she was 'aving both hands squeezed at once under the table and could 'ardly get a bite in edgeways.

Old Bill lit his pipe arter supper, and then, taking another glass o' beer, he told 'em about the cook dreaming of his accident three days afore it happened. They couldn't 'ardly believe it at fust, but when he went on to tell 'em the other things the cook 'ad dreamt, and that everything 'ad 'appened just as he dreamt it, they all edged away from the cook and sat staring at him with their mouths open.

"And that ain't the worst of it," ses Bill.

"That's enough for one night, Bill," ses Joseph,

The Dreamer

who was staring at Bert Simmons as though he could eat him. "Besides, I believe it was on'y chance. When cook told you 'is dream it made you nervous, and that's why you fell."

"Nervous be blowed!" ses Bill; and then he told 'em about the dream he 'ad heard while he was laying in 'is bunk.

Bill's sister gave a scream when he 'ad finished, and Emily, wot was sitting next to Joseph, got up with a shiver and went and sat next to Bert Simmons and squeezed his coat-sleeve.

"It's all nonsense!" ses Joseph, starting up. "And if it wasn't, true love would run the risk. I ain't afraid!"

"It's too much to ask a gal," ses Bert Simmons, shaking his 'ead.

"I couldn't dream of it," ses Emily. "Wot's the use of being married for a week? Look at uncle's leg—that's enough for me!"

They all talked at once then, and Joseph tried all he could to persuade Emily to prove to the cook that 'is dreams didn't always come true; but it was no good. Emily said she wouldn't marry 'im if he 'ad a million a year, and her aunt and uncle backed her up in it—to say nothing of Bert Simmons.

"I'll go up and get your presents, Joseph," she

The Dreamer

ses; and she ran upstairs afore anybody could stop her.

Joseph sat there as if he was dazed, while everybody gave 'im good advice, and said 'ow thankful he ought to be that the cook 'ad saved him by 'is dreaming. And by and by Emily came downstairs agin with the presents he 'ad given 'er and put them on the table in front of 'im.

"There's everything there but that little silver brooch you gave me, Joseph," she ses, "and I lost that the other evening when I was out with— with—for a walk."

Joseph tried to speak, but couldn't.

"It was six-and-six, 'cos I was with you when you bought it," ses Emily; "and as I've lost it, it's on'y fair I should pay for it."

She put down 'arf a sovereign with the presents, and Joseph sat staring at it as if he 'ad never seen one afore.

"And you needn't mind about the change, Joseph," ses Emily; "that'll 'elp to make up for your disappointment."

Old Bill tried to turn things off with a bit of a laugh. "Why, you're made o' money, Emily," he ses.

"Ah! I haven't told you yet," ses Emily, smiling at him; "that's a little surprise I was keeping

The Dreamer

for you. Aunt Emma — pore Aunt Emma, I should say—died while you was away and left me all 'er furniture and two hundred pounds."

Joseph made a choking noise in his throat and then 'e got up, leaving the presents and the 'arf-sovereign on the table, and stood by the door, staring at them.

" Good-night all," he ses. Then he went to the front door and opened it, and arter standing there a moment came back as though he 'ad forgotten something.

" Are you coming along now? " he ses to the cook.

" Not just yet," ses the cook, very quick.

" I'll wait outside for you, then," ses Joseph, grinding his teeth. " Don't be long."

ANGELS' VISITS

Angels' Visits

MR. WILLIAM JOBLING leaned against his door-post, smoking. The evening air, pleasant in its coolness after the heat of the day, caressed his shirt-sleeved arms. Children played noisily in the long, dreary street, and an organ sounded faintly in the distance. To Mr. Jobling, who had just consumed three herrings and a pint and a half of strong tea, the scene was delightful. He blew a little cloud of smoke in the air, and with half-closed eyes corrected his first impression as to the tune being played round the corner.

" Bill! " cried the voice of Mrs. Jobling, who was washing-up in the tiny scullery.

" 'Ullo! " responded Mr. Jobling, gruffly.

" You've been putting your wet teaspoon in the sugar-basin, and — well, I declare, if you haven't done it again."

" Done what? " inquired her husband, hunching his shoulders.

Angels' Visits

"Putting your herringy knife in the butter. Well, you can eat it now; I won't. A lot of good me slaving from morning to night and buying good food when you go and spoil it like that."

Mr. Jobling removed the pipe from his mouth. "Not so much of it," he commanded. "I like butter with a little flavor to it. As for your slaving all day, you ought to come to the works for a week; you'd know what slavery was then."

Mrs. Jobling permitted herself a thin, derisive cackle, drowned hurriedly in a clatter of tea-cups as her husband turned and looked angrily up the little passage.

"Nag! nag! nag!" said Mr. Jobling.

He paused expectantly.

"Nag! nag! nag! from morning till night," he resumed. "It begins in the morning and it goes on till bedtime."

"It's a pity——" began Mrs. Jobling.

"Hold your tongue," said her husband, sternly; "I don't want any of your back answers. It goes on all day long up to bedtime, and last night I laid awake for two hours listening to you nagging in your sleep."

He paused again.

"Nagging in your sleep," he repeated.

There was no reply.

" Two hours ! " he said, invitingly; " two whole hours, without a stop."

" I 'ope it done you good," retorted his wife. " I noticed you did wipe one foot when you come in to-night."

Mr. Jobling denied the charge hotly, and, by way of emphasizing his denial, raised his foot and sent the mat flying along the passage. Honor satisfied, he returned to the door-post and, looking idly out on the street again, exchanged a few desultory remarks with Mr. Joe Brown, who, with his hands in his pockets, was balancing himself with great skill on the edge of the curb opposite.

His gaze wandered from Mr. Brown to a young and rather stylishly-dressed woman who was approaching—a tall, good-looking girl with a slight limp, whose hat encountered unspoken feminine criticism at every step. Their eyes met as she came up, and recognition flashed suddenly into both faces.

" Fancy seeing you here ! " said the girl. " Well, this is a pleasant surprise."

She held out her hand, and Mr. Jobling, with a fierce glance at Mr. Brown, who was not behaving, shook it respectfully.

" I'm so glad to see you again," said the girl; " I know I didn't thank you half enough the other night, but I was too upset."

" Don't mention it," said Mr. Jobling, in a voice the humility of which was in strong contrast to the expression with which he was regarding the antics of Mr. Brown, as that gentleman wafted kisses to the four winds of heaven.

There was a pause, broken by a short, dry cough from the parlor window. The girl, who was almost touching the sill, started nervously.

" It's only my missis," said Mr. Jobling.

The girl turned and gazed in at the window. Mr. Jobling, with the stem of his pipe, performed a brief ceremony of introduction.

" Good-evening," said Mrs. Jobling, in a thin voice. " I don't know who you are, but I s'pose my 'usband does."

" I met him the other night," said the girl, with a bright smile; " I slipped on a piece of peel or something and fell, and he was passing and helped me up."

Mrs. Jobling coughed again. " First I've heard of it," she remarked.

" I forgot to tell you," said Mr. Jobling, carelessly. " I hope you wasn't hurt much, miss? "

" I twisted my ankle a bit, that's all," said the girl; " it's painful when I walk."

" Painful now? " inquired Mr. Jobling, in concern.

The girl nodded. " A little; not very."

Mr. Jobling hesitated; the contortions of Mr. Brown's face as he strove to make a wink carry across the road would have given pause to a bolder man; and twice his wife's husky little cough had sounded from the window.

" I s'pose you wouldn't like to step inside and rest for five minutes? " he said, slowly.

" Oh, thank you," said the girl, gratefully; " I should like to. It — it really is very painful. I ought not to have walked so far."

She limped in behind Mr. Jobling, and after bowing to Mrs. Jobling sank into the easy-chair with a sigh of relief and looked keenly round the room. Mr. Jobling disappeared, and his wife flushed darkly as he came back with his coat on and his hair wet from combing. An awkward silence ensued.

" How strong your husband is! " said the girl, clasping her hands impulsively.

" Is he? " said Mrs. Jobling.

" He lifted me up as though I had been a feather," responded the girl. " He just put his arm round my waist and had me on my feet before I knew where I was."

" Round your waist? " repeated Mrs. Jobling.

" Where else should I put it? " broke in her husband, with sudden violence.

Angels' Visits

His wife made no reply, but sat gazing in a hostile fashion at the bold, dark eyes and stylish hat of the visitor.

"I should like to be strong," said the latter, smiling agreeably over at Mr. Jobling.

"When I was younger," said that gratified man, "I can assure you I didn't know my own strength, as the saying is. I used to hurt people just in play like, without knowing it. I used to have a hug like a bear."

"Fancy being hugged like that!" said the girl. "How awful!" she added, hastily, as she caught the eye of the speechless Mrs. Jobling.

"Like a bear," repeated Mr. Jobling, highly pleased at the impression he had made. "I'm pretty strong now; there ain't many as I'm afraid of."

He bent his arm and thoughtfully felt his biceps, and Mrs. Jobling almost persuaded herself that she must be dreaming, as she saw the girl lean forward and pinch Mr. Jobling's arm. Mr. Jobling was surprised too, but he had the presence of mind to bend the other.

"Enormous!" said the girl, "and as hard as iron. What a prize-fighter you'd have made!"

"He don't want to do no prize-fighting," said Mrs. Jobling, recovering her speech; "he's a respectable married man."

Angels' Visits

Mr. Jobling shook his head over lost opportunities. " I'm too old," he remarked.

" He's forty-seven," said his wife.

" Best age for a man, in my opinion," said the girl; " just entering his prime. And a man is as old as he feels, you know."

Mr. Jobling nodded acquiescence and observed that he always felt about twenty-two; a state of affairs which he ascribed to regular habits, and a great partiality for the company of young people.

" I was just twenty-two when I married," he mused, " and my missis was just six months——"

" You leave my age alone," interrupted his wife, trembling with passion. " I'm not so fond of telling my age to strangers."

" You told mine," retorted Mr. Jobling, " and nobody asked you to do that. Very free you was in coming out with mine."

" I ain't the only one that's free," breathed the quivering Mrs. Jobling. " I 'ope your ankle is better? " she added, turning to the visitor.

" Much better, thank you," was the reply.

" Got far to go? " queried Mrs. Jobling.

The girl nodded. " But I shall take a tram at the end of the street," she said, rising.

Mr. Jobling rose too, and all that he had ever heard or read about etiquette came crowding into his mind. A weekly journal patronized by his wife had three columns regularly, but he taxed his memory in vain for any instructions concerning brown-eyed strangers with sprained ankles. He felt that the path of duty led to the tram-lines. In a somewhat blundering fashion he proffered his services; the girl accepted them as a matter of course.

Mrs. Jobling, with lips tightly compressed, watched them from the door. The girl, limping slightly, walked along with the utmost composure, but the bearing of her escort betokened a mind fully conscious of the scrutiny of the street.

He returned in about half an hour, and having this time to run the gauntlet of the street alone, entered with a mien which caused his wife's complaints to remain unspoken. The cough of Mr. Brown, a particularly contagious one, still rang in his ears, and he sat for some time in fierce silence.

" I see her on the tram," he said, at last. " Her name's Robinson—Miss Robinson."

" In-deed! " said his wife.

" Seems a nice sort o' girl," said Mr. Jobling, carelessly. " She's took quite a fancy to you."

" I'm sure I'm much obliged to her," retorted his wife.

" So I—so I asked her to give you a look in

Angels' Visits

"He astonished Mrs. Jobling next day by the gift of a
geranium."

now and then," continued Mr. Jobling, filling his pipe with great care, " and she said she would. It'll cheer you up a bit."

Mrs. Jobling bit her lip and, although she had never felt more fluent in her life, said nothing. Her husband lit his pipe, and after a rapid glance in her direction took up an old newspaper and began to read.

He astonished Mrs. Jobling next day by the gift of a geranium in full bloom. Surprise impeded her utterance, but she thanked him at last with some warmth, and after a little deliberation decided to put it in the bedroom.

Mr. Jobling looked like a man who has suddenly discovered a flaw in his calculations. " I was thinking of the front parlor winder," he said, at last.

" It'll get more sun upstairs," said his wife.

She took the pot in her arms, and disappeared. Her surprise when she came down again and found Mr. Jobling rearranging the furniture, and even adding a choice ornament or two from the kitchen, was too elaborate to escape his notice.

" Been going to do it for some time," he remarked.

Mrs. Jobling left the room and strove with herself in the scullery. She came back pale of face and with a gleam in her eye which her husband was too busy to notice.

" It'll never look much till we get a new hearth-rug," she said, shaking her head. " They've got one at Jackson's that would be just the thing; and they've got a couple of tall pink vases that would brighten up the fireplace wonderful. They're going for next to nothing, too."

Mr. Jobling's reply took the form of uncouth and disagreeable growlings. After that phase had passed he sat for some time with his hand placed protectingly in his trouser-pocket. Finally, in a fierce voice, he inquired the cost.

Ten minutes later, in a state fairly evenly di-vided between pleasure and fury, Mrs. Jobling departed with the money. Wild yearnings for courage that would enable her to spend the money differently, and confront the dismayed Mr. Jobling in a new hat and jacket, possessed her on the way; but they were only yearnings, twenty-five years' experience of her husband's temper being a suffi-cient safeguard.

Miss Robinson came in the day after as they were sitting down to tea. Mr. Jobling, who was in his shirt-sleeves, just had time to disappear as the girl passed the window. His wife let her in, and after five remarks about the weather sat listening in grim pleasure to the efforts of Mr. Jobling to find his coat. He found it at last, under a chair cushion, and, somewhat red of face, entered the room and greeted the visitor.

Conversation was at first rather awkward. The girl's eyes wandered round the room and paused in astonishment on the pink vases; the beauty of the rug also called for notice.

"Yes, they're pretty good," said Mr. Jobling, much gratified by her approval.

"Beautiful," murmured the girl. "What a thing it is to have money!" she said, wistfully.

"I could do with some," said Mr. Jobling, with jocularity. He helped himself to bread and butter and began to discuss money and how to spend it. His ideas favored retirement and a nice little place in the country.

"I wonder you don't do it," said the girl, softly.

Mr. Jobling laughed. "Gingell and Watson don't pay on those lines," he said. "We do the work and they take the money."

"It's always the way," said the girl, indignantly; "they have all the luxuries, and the men who make the money for them all the hardships. I seem to know the name Gingell and Watson. I wonder where I've seen it?"

Angels' Visits

" In the paper, p'r'aps," said Mr. Jobling.

" Advertising? " asked the girl.

Mr. Jobling shook his head. " Robbery," he replied, seriously. " It was in last week's paper. Somebody got to the safe and got away with nine hundred pounds in gold and bank-notes."

" I remember now," said the girl, nodding. " Did they catch them? "

" No, and not likely to," was the reply.

Miss Robinson opened her big eyes and looked round with an air of pretty defiance. " I am glad of it," she said.

"Glad?" said Mrs. Jobling, involuntarily break-ing a self-imposed vow of silence. " Glad? "

The girl nodded. " I like pluck," she said, with a glance in the direction of Mr. Jobling; " and, besides, whoever took it had as much right to it as Gingell and Watson; they didn't earn it."

Mrs. Jobling, appalled at such ideas, glanced at her husband to see how he received them. " The man's a thief," she said, with great energy, " and he won't enjoy his gains."

" I dare say—I dare say he'll enjoy it right enough," said Mr. Jobling, " if he ain't caught, that is."

" I believe he is the sort of man I should like," declared Miss Robinson, obstinately.

"I dare say," said Mrs. Jobling; "and I've no doubt he'd like you. Birds of a——"

"That'll do," said her husband, peremptorily; "that's enough about it. The guv'nors can afford to lose it; that's one comfort."

He leaned over as the girl asked for more sugar and dropped a spoonful in her cup, expressing surprise that she should like her tea so sweet. Miss Robinson, denying the sweetness, proffered her cup in proof, and Mrs. Jobling sat watching with blazing eyes the antics of her husband as he sipped at it.

"Sweets to the sweet," he said, gallantly, as he handed it back.

Miss Robinson pouted, and, raising the cup to her lips, gazed ardently at him over the rim. Mr. Jobling, who certainly felt not more than twenty-two that evening, stole her cake and received in return a rap from a teaspoon. Mr. Jobling retaliated, and Mrs. Jobling, unable to eat, sat looking on in helpless fury at little arts of fascination which she had discarded—at Mr. Jobling's earnest request—soon after their marriage.

By dint of considerable self-control, aided by an occasional glance from her husband, she managed to preserve her calm until he returned from seeing the visitor to her tram. Then her pent-up

Angels' Visits

" They offered Mrs. Jobling her choice of at least a hundred plans
for bringing him to his senses."

feelings found vent. Quietly scornful at first, she soon waxed hysterical over his age and figure. Tears followed as she bade him remember what a good wife she had been to him, loudly claiming that any other woman would have poisoned him long ago. Speedily finding that tears were of no avail, and that Mr. Jobling seemed to regard them rather as a tribute to his worth than otherwise, she gave way to fury, and, in a fine, but unpunctuated passage, told him her exact opinion of Miss Robinson.

" It's no good carrying on like that," said Mr. Jobling, magisterially, " and, what's more, I won't have it."

" Walking into my house and making eyes at my 'usband," stormed his wife.

" So long as I don't make eyes at her there's no harm done," retorted Mr. Jobling. " I can't help her taking a fancy to me, poor thing."

" I'd poor thing her," said his wife.

" She's to be pitied," said Mr. Jobling, sternly. " I know how she feels. She can't help herself, but she'll get over it in time. I don't suppose she thinks for a moment we have noticed her—her— her liking for me, and I'm not going to have her feelings hurt."

" What about my feelings? " demanded his wife.

Angels' Visits

"*You* have got me," Mr. Jobling reminded her.

The nine points of the law was Mrs. Jobling's only consolation for the next few days. Neighboring matrons, exchanging sympathy for information, wished, strangely enough, that Mr. Jobling was their husband. Failing that they offered Mrs. Jobling her choice of at least a hundred plans for bringing him to his senses.

Mr. Jobling, who was a proud man, met their hostile glances as he passed to and from his work with scorn, until a day came when the hostility vanished and gave place to smiles. Never so many people in the street, he thought, as he returned from work; certainly never so many smiles. People came hurriedly from their back premises to smile at him, and, as he reached his door, Mr. Joe Brown opposite had all the appearance of a human sunbeam. Tired of smiling faces, he yearned for that of his wife. She came out of the kitchen and met him with a look of sly content. The perplexed Mr. Jobling eyed her morosely.

"What are you laughing at me for?" he demanded.

"I wasn't laughing at you," said his wife.

She went back into the kitchen and sang blithely as she bustled over the preparations for tea. Her voice was feeble, but there was a triumphant effectiveness about the high notes which perplexed the listener sorely. He seated himself in the new easy-chair—procured to satisfy the supposed æsthetic tastes of Miss Robinson—and stared at the window.

"You seem very happy all of a sudden," he growled, as his wife came in with the tray.

"Well, why shouldn't I be?" inquired Mrs. Jobling. "I've got everything to make me so."

Mr. Jobling looked at her in undisguised amazement.

"New easy-chair, new vases, and a new hearth-rug," explained his wife, looking round the room. "Did you order that little table you said you would?"

"Yes," growled Mr. Jobling.

"Pay for it?" inquired his wife, with a trace of anxiety.

"Yes," said Mr. Jobling again.

Mrs. Jobling's face relaxed. "I shouldn't like to lose it at the last moment," she said. "You 'ave been good to me lately, Bill; buying all these nice things. There's not many women have got such a thoughtful husband as what I have."

"Have you gone dotty? or what?" inquired her bewildered husband.

"It's no wonder people like you," pursued Mrs.

Jobling, ignoring the question, and smiling again as she placed three chairs at the table. " I'll wait a minute or two before I soak the tea; I expect Miss Robinson won't be long, and she likes it fresh."

Mr. Jobling, to conceal his amazement and to obtain a little fresh air walked out of the room and opened the front door.

" Cheer oh! " said the watchful Mr. Brown, with a benignant smile.

Mr. Jobling scowled at him.

" It's all right," said Mr. Brown. " You go in and set down; I'm watching for her."

He nodded reassuringly, and, not having curiosity enough to accept the other's offer and step across the road and see what he would get, shaded his eyes with his hand and looked with exaggerated anxiety up the road. Mr. Jobling, heavy of brow, returned to the parlor and looked hard at his wife.

" She's late," said Mrs. Jobling, glancing at the clock. " I do hope she's all right, but I should feel anxious about her if she was my gal. It's a dangerous life."

" Dangerous life! " said Mr. Jobling, roughly. " What's a dangerous life? "

" Why, hers," replied his wife, with a nervous smile. " Joe Brown told me. He followed her 'ome last night, and this morning he found out all about her."

The mention of Mr. Brown's name caused Mr. Jobling at first to assume an air of indifference; but curiosity overpowered him.

"What lies has he been telling?" he demanded.

"I don't think it's a lie, Bill," said his wife, mildly. "Putting two and two——"

"What did he say?" cried Mr. Jobling, raising his voice.

"He said, 'She—she's a lady detective,'" stammered Mrs. Jobling, putting her handkerchief to her unruly mouth.

"A tec!" repeated her husband. "A lady tec?"

Mrs. Jobling nodded. "Yes, Bill. She—she —she——"

"Well?" said Mr. Jobling, in exasperation.

"She's being employed by Gingell and Watson," said his wife.

Mr. Jobling sprang to his feet, and with scarlet face and clinched fists strove to assimilate the information and all its meaning.

"What—what did she come here for? Do you mean to tell me she thinks *I* took the money?" he said, huskily, after a long pause.

Mrs. Jobling bent before the storm. "I think she took a fancy to you, Bill," she said, timidly.

Angels' Visits

Mr. Jobling appeared to swallow something; then he took a step nearer to her. " You let me see you laugh again, that's all," he said, fiercely. " As for that Jezzybill——"

" There she is," said his wife, as a knock sounded at the door. " Don't say anything to hurt her feelings, Bill. You said she was to be pitied. And it must be a hard life to 'ave to go round and flatter old married men. I shouldn't like it."

Mr. Jobling, past speech, stood and glared at her. Then, with an inarticulate cry, he rushed to the front door and flung it open. Miss Robinson, fresh and bright, stood smiling outside. Within easy distance a little group of neighbors were making conversation, while opposite Mr. Brown awaited events.

" What d'you want? " demanded Mr. Jobling, harshly.

Miss Robinson, who had put out her hand, drew it back and gave him a swift glance. His red face and knitted brows told their own story.

" Oh! " she said, with a winning smile, " will you please tell Mrs. Jobling that I can't come to tea with her this evening? "

" Isn't there anything else you'd like to say? " inquired Mr. Jobling, disdainfully, as she turned away.

Angels' Visits

The girl paused and appeared to reflect. "You can say that I am sorry to miss an amusing evening," she said, regarding him steadily. "Good-by."

Mr. Jobling slammed the door.

A CIRCULAR TOUR

A Circular Tour

ILLNESS? said the night watchman, slowly. Yes, sailormen get ill sometimes, but not 'aving the time for it that other people have, and there being no doctors at sea, they soon pick up agin. Ashore, if a man's ill he goes to a horse-pittle and 'as a nice nurse to wait on 'im; at sea the mate comes down and tells 'im that there is nothing the matter with 'im, and asks 'im if he ain't ashamed of 'imself. The only mate I ever knew that showed any feeling was one who 'ad been a doctor and 'ad gone to sea to better 'imself. He didn't believe in medicine; his idea was to cut things out, and he was so kind and tender, and so fond of 'is little box of knives and saws, that you wouldn't ha' thought anybody could 'ave had the 'art to say "no" to him. But they did. I remember 'im getting up at four o'clock one morning to cut a man's leg off, and at ha'-past three the chap was sitting up aloft with four pairs o' trousers on and a belaying-pin in his 'and.

A Circular Tour

One chap I knew, Joe Summers by name, got so sick o' work one v'y'ge that he went mad. Not dangerous mad, mind you. Just silly. One thing he did was to pretend that the skipper was 'is little boy, and foller 'im up unbeknown and pat his 'ead. At last, to pacify him, the old man pretended that he was 'is little boy, and a precious handful of a boy he was too, I can tell you. Fust of all he showed 'is father 'ow they wrestled at school, and arter that he showed 'im 'ow he 'arf killed another boy in fifteen rounds. Leastways he was going to, but arter seven rounds Joe's madness left 'im all of a sudden and he was as right as ever he was.

Sailormen are more frequent ill ashore than at sea; they've got more time for it, I s'pose. Old Sam Small, a man you may remember by name as a pal o' mine, got ill once, and, like most 'ealthy men who get a little something the matter with 'em, he made sure 'e was dying. He was sharing a bedroom with Ginger Dick and Peter Russet at the time, and early one morning he woke up groaning with a chill or something which he couldn't account for, but which Ginger thought might ha' been partly caused through 'im sleeping in the fireplace.

"Is that you, Sam?" ses Ginger, waking up

with the noise and rubbing his eyes. "Wot's the matter?"

"I'm dying," ses Sam, with another awful groan. "Good-by, Ginger."

"Goo'-by," ses Ginger, turning over and falling fast asleep agin.

Old Sam picked 'imself up arter two or three tries, and then he staggered over to Peter Russet's bed and sat on the foot of it, groaning, until Peter woke up very cross and tried to push 'im off with his feet.

"I'm dying, Peter," ses Sam, and 'e rolled over and buried his face in the bed-clo'es and kicked. Peter Russet, who was a bit scared, sat up in bed and called for Ginger, and arter he 'ad called pretty near a dozen times Ginger 'arf woke up and asked 'im wot was the matter.

"Poor old Sam's dying," ses Peter.

"I know," ses Ginger, laying down and cuddling into the piller agin. "He told me just now. I've bid 'im good-by."

Peter Russet asked 'im where his 'art was, but Ginger was asleep agin. Then Peter sat up in bed and tried to comfort Sam, and listened while 'e told 'im wot it felt like to die. How 'e was 'ot and cold all over, burning and shivering, with pains in his inside that he couldn't describe if 'e tried.

A Circular Tour

"It'll soon be over, Sam," ses Peter, kindly, "and all your troubles will be at an end. While me and Ginger are knocking about at sea trying to earn a crust o' bread to keep ourselves alive, you'll be quiet and at peace."

Sam groaned. "I don't like being too quiet," he ses. "I was always one for a bit o' fun—innercent fun."

Peter coughed.

"You and Ginger 'av been good pals," ses Sam; "it's hard to go and leave you."

"We've all got to go some time or other, Sam," ses Peter, soothing-like. "It's a wonder to me, with your habits, that you've lasted as long as you 'ave."

"My *habits*?" ses Sam, sitting up all of a sudden. "Why, you monkey-faced son of a sea-cook, for two pins I'd chuck you out of the winder."

"Don't talk like that on your death-bed," ses Peter, very shocked.

Sam was going to answer 'im sharp agin, but just then 'e got a pain which made 'im roll about on the bed and groan to such an extent that Ginger woke up agin and got out o' bed.

"Pore old Sam!" he ses, walking across the room and looking at 'im. "'Ave you got any pain anywhere?"

A Circular Tour

"*Pain?*" ses Sam. "Pain? I'm a mask o' pains all over."

Ginger and Peter looked at 'im and shook their 'eds, and then they went a little way off and talked about 'im in whispers.

"He looks 'arf dead now," ses Peter, coming back and staring at 'im. "Let's take 'is clothes off, Ginger; it's more decent to die with 'em off."

"I think I'll 'ave a doctor," ses Sam, in a faint voice.

"You're past doctors, Sam," ses Ginger, in a kind voice.

"Better 'ave your last moments in peace," ses Peter, "and keep your money in your trouser-pockets."

"You go and fetch a doctor, you murderers," ses Sam, groaning, as Peter started to undress 'im. "Go on, else I'll haunt you with my ghost."

Ginger tried to talk to 'im about the sin o' wasting money, but it was all no good, and arter telling Peter wot to do in case Sam died afore he come back, he went off. He was gone about 'arf an hour, and then he come back with a sandy-'aired young man with red eyelids and a black bag.

"Am I dying, sir?" ses Sam, arter the doctor 'ad listened to his lungs and his 'art and prodded 'im all over.

A Circular Tour

"We're all dying," ses the doctor, "only some of us'll go sooner than others."

"Will he last the day, sir?" ses Ginger.

The doctor looked at Sam agin, and Sam held 'is breath while 'e waited for him to answer. "Yes," ses the doctor at last, "if he does just wot I tell him and takes the medicine I send 'im."

He wasn't in the room 'arf an hour altogether, and he charged pore Sam a shilling; but wot 'urt Sam even more than that was to hear 'im go off downstairs whistling as cheerful as if there wasn't a dying man within a 'undred miles.

Peter and Ginger Dick took turns to be with Sam that morning, but in the arternoon the land-lady's mother, an old lady who was almost as fat as Sam 'imself, came up to look arter 'im a bit. She sat on a chair by the side of 'is bed and tried to amuse 'im by telling 'im of all the death-beds she'd been at, and partikler of one man, the living image of Sam, who passed away in his sleep. It was past ten o'clock when Peter and Ginger came 'ome, but they found pore Sam still awake and sitting up in bed holding 'is eyes open with his fingers.

Sam had another shilling's-worth the next day, and 'is medicine was changed for the worse. If anything he seemed a trifle better, but the land-

278

A Circular Tour

"She asked 'im whether 'e'd got a fancy for any partikler spot to
be buried in."

A Circular Tour

lady's mother, wot came up to nurse 'im agin, said it was a bad sign, and that people often brightened up just afore the end. She asked 'im whether 'e'd got a fancy for any partikler spot to be buried in, and, talking about wot a lot o' people 'ad been buried alive, said she'd ask the doctor to cut Sam's 'ead off to prevent mistakes. She got quite annoyed with Sam for saying, supposing there *was* a mistake and he came round in the middle of it, how'd he feel? and said there was no satisfying some people, do wot you would.

At the end o' six days Sam was still alive and losing a shilling a day, to say nothing of buying 'is own beef-tea and such-like. Ginger said it was fair highway robbery, and tried to persuade Sam to go to a 'orsepittle, where he'd 'ave lovely nurses to wait on 'im hand and foot, and wouldn't keep 'is best friends awake of a night making 'orrible noises.

Sam didn't take kindly to the idea at fust, but as the doctor forbid 'im to get up, although he felt much better, and his money was wasting away, he gave way at last, and at seven o'clock one evening he sent Ginger off to fetch a cab to take 'im to the London Horsepittle. Sam said something about putting 'is clothes on, but Peter Russet said the horsepittle would be more likely to take him in

if he went in the blanket and counterpane, and at
last Sam gave way. Ginger and Peter helped 'im
downstairs, and the cabman laid hold o' one end
o' the blanket as they got to the street-door, under
the idea that he was helping, and very near gave
Sam another chill.

"Keep your hair on," he ses, as Sam started on
'im. "It'll be three-and-six for the fare, and I'll
take the money now."

"You'll 'ave it when you get there," ses Ginger.

"I'll 'ave it now," ses the cabman. "I 'ad a
fare die on the way once afore."

Ginger—who was minding Sam's money for
'im because there wasn't a pocket in the counterpane—paid 'im, and the cab started. It jolted
and rattled over the stones, but Sam said the air
was doing 'im good. He kept 'is pluck up until
they got close to the horsepittle, and then 'e got
nervous. And 'e got more nervous when the cabman got down off 'is box and put his 'ed in at the
winder and spoke to 'im.

"'Ave you got any partikler fancy for the London Horsepittle?" he ses.

"No," ses Sam. "Why?"

"Well, I s'pose it don't matter, if wot your
mate ses is true—that you're dying," ses the cabman.

"Wot d'ye mean?" says Sam.

A Circular Tour

"Nothing," ses the cabman; "only, fust and last, I s'pose I've driven five 'undred people to that 'orsepittle, and only one ever came out agin —and he was smuggled out in a bread-basket."

Sam's flesh began to creep all over.

"It's a pity they don't 'ave the same rules as Charing Cross Horsepittle," ses the cabman. "The doctors 'ave five pounds apiece for every patient that gets well there, and the consequence is they ain't 'ad the blinds down for over five months."

"Drive me there," ses Sam.

"It's a long way," ses the cabman, shaking his 'ed, "and it 'ud cost you another 'arf dollar. S'pose you give the London a try?"

"You drive to Charing Cross," ses Sam, telling Ginger to give 'im the 'arf-dollar. "And look sharp; these things ain't as warm as they might be."

The cabman turned his 'orse round and set off agin, singing. The cab stopped once or twice for a little while, and then it stopped for quite a long time, and the cabman climbed down off 'is box and came to the winder agin.

"I'm sorry, mate," he ses, "but did you see me speak to that party just now?"

"The one you flicked with your whip?" ses Ginger.

A Circular Tour

"No; he was speaking to me," ses the cabman. "The last one, I mean."

"Wot about it?" ses Peter.

"He's the under-porter at the horsepittle," ses the cabman, spitting; "and he tells me that every bed is bung full, and two patients apiece in some of 'em."

"I don't mind sleeping two in a bed," ses Sam, who was very tired and cold.

"No," ses the cabman, looking at 'im; "but wot about the other one?"

"Well, what's to be done?" ses Peter.

"You might go to Guy's," ses the cabman; "that's as good as Charing Cross."

"I b'lieve you're telling a pack o' lies," ses Ginger.

"Come out o' my cab," ses the cabman, very fierce. "Come on, all of you. Out you get."

Ginger and Peter was for getting out, but Sam wouldn't 'ear of it. It was bad enough being wrapped up in a blanket in a cab, without being turned out in 'is bare feet on the pavement, and at last Ginger apologized to the cabman by saying 'e supposed if he was a liar he couldn't 'elp it. The cabman collected three shillings more to go to Guy's 'orsepittle, and, arter a few words with Ginger, climbed up on 'is box and drove off agin.

A Circular Tour

They were all rather tired of the cab by this time, and, going over Waterloo Bridge, Ginger began to feel uncommon thirsty, and, leaning out of the winder, he told the cabman to pull up for a drink. He was so long about it that Ginger began to think he was bearing malice, but just as he was going to tell 'im agin, the cab pulled up in a quiet little street opposite a small pub. Ginger Dick and Peter went in and 'ad something and brought one out for Sam. They 'ad another arter that, and Ginger, getting 'is good temper back agin, asked the cabman to 'ave one.

" Look lively about it, Ginger," ses Sam, very sharp. " You forget 'ow ill I am."

Ginger said they wouldn't be two seconds, and, the cabman calling a boy to mind his 'orse, they went inside. It was a quiet little place, but very cosey, and Sam, peeping out of the winder, could see all three of 'em leaning against the bar and making themselves comfortable. Twice he made the boy go in to hurry them up, and all the notice they took was to go on at the boy for leaving the horse.

Pore old Sam sat there hugging 'imself in the bed-clo'es, and getting wilder and wilder. He couldn't get out of the cab, and 'e couldn't call to them for fear of people coming up and staring at 'im. Ginger, smiling all over with 'appiness, had got a big cigar on and was pretending to pinch the barmaid's flowers, and Peter and the cabman was talking to some other chaps there. The only change Sam 'ad was when the boy walked the 'orse up and down the road.

He sat there for an hour and then 'e sent the boy in agin. This time the cabman lost 'is temper, and, arter chasing the boy up the road, gave a young feller twopence to take 'is place and promised 'im another twopence when he came out. Sam tried to get a word with 'im as 'e passed, but he wouldn't listen, and it was pretty near 'arf an hour later afore they all came out, talking and laughing.

"Now for the 'orsepittle," ses Ginger, opening the door. "Come on, Peter; don't keep pore old Sam waiting all night."

"'Arf a tic," ses the cabman, "'arf a tic; there's five shillings for waiting, fust."

"*Wot?*" ses Ginger, staring at 'im. "Arter giving you all them drinks?"

"Five shillings," ses the cabman; "two hours' waiting at half a crown an hour. That's the proper charge."

Ginger thought 'e was joking at fust, and when he found 'e wasn't he called 'im all the names he could think of, while Peter Russet stood by smiling and trying to think where 'e was and wot it was all about.

"Pay 'im the five bob, Ginger, and 'ave done with it," ses pore Sam, at last. "I shall never get to the horsepittle at this rate."

"Cert'inly not," ses Ginger, "not if we stay 'ere all night."

"Pay 'im the five bob," ses Sam, raising 'is voice; "it's my money."

"You keep quiet," ses Ginger, "and speak when your spoke to. Get inside, Peter."

Peter, wot was standing by blinking and smiling, misunderstood 'im, and went back inside the pub. Ginger went arter 'im to fetch 'im back, and hearing a noise turned round and saw the cabman pulling Sam out o' the cab. He was just in time to shove 'im back agin, and for the next two or three minutes 'im and the cabman was 'ard at it. Sam was too busy holding 'is clothes on to do much, and twice the cabman got 'im 'arf out, and twice Ginger got him back agin and bumped 'im back in 'is seat and shut the door. Then they both stopped and took breath.

"We'll see which gets tired fust," ses Ginger. "Hold the door inside, Sam."

The cabman looked at 'im, and then 'e climbed

up on to 'is seat and, just as Ginger ran back for Peter Russet, drove off at full speed.

Pore Sam leaned back in 'is seat panting and trying to wrap 'imself up better in the counterpane, which 'ad got torn in the struggle. They went through street arter street, and 'e was just thinking of a nice warm bed and a kind nurse listening to all 'is troubles when 'e found they was going over London Bridge.

" You've passed it," he ses, putting his 'ead out of the winder.

The cabman took no notice, and afore Sam could think wot to make of it they was in the Whitechapel Road, and arter that, although Sam kept putting his 'ead out of the winder and asking 'im questions, they kept going through a lot o' little back streets until 'e began to think the cabman 'ad lost 'is way. They stopped at last in a dark little road, in front of a brick wall, and then the cabman got down and opened a door and led his 'orse and cab into a yard.

" Do you call this Guy's Horsepittle ? " ses Sam.

" Hullo ! " ses the cabman. " Why, I thought I put you out o' my cab once."

" I'll give you five minutes to drive me to the 'orsepittle," ses Sam. " Arter that I shall go for the police."

A Circular Tour

" All right," ses the cabman, taking his 'orse out and leading it into a stable. " Mind you don't catch cold."

He lighted a lantern and began to look arter the 'orse, and pore Sam sat there getting colder and colder and wondering wot 'e was going to do.

" I shall give you in charge for kidnapping me," he calls out very loud.

" Kidnapping? " ses the cabman. " Who do you think wants to kidnap you? The gate's open, and you can go as soon as you like."

Sam climbed out of the cab, and holding up the counterpane walked across the yard in 'is bare feet to the stable. " Well, will you drive me 'ome? " he ses.

" Cert'inly not," ses the cabman; " I'm going 'ome myself now. It's time you went, 'cos I'm going to lock up."

" 'Ow can I go like this? " ses Sam, bursting with passion. " Ain't you got any sense? "

" Well, wot are you going to do? " ses the cabman, picking 'is teeth with a bit o' straw.

" Wot would you do if you was me? " ses Sam, calming down a bit and trying to speak civil.

" Well, if I was you," said the cabman, speaking very slow, " I should be more perlite to begin with;

A Circular Tour

" ' All right,' ses the cabman, taking his 'orse out and leading it into a stable.   'Mind you don't catch cold.' "

you accused me just now—me, a 'ard-working man
—o' kidnapping you."

" It was only my fun," ses Sam, very quick.

" I ain't kidnapping you, am I? " ses the cabman.

" Cert'inly not," ses Sam.

" Well, then," ses the cabman, " if I was you I
should pay 'arf a crown for a night's lodging in
this nice warm stable, and in the morning I should
ask the man it belongs to—that's me—to go up
to my lodging with a letter, asking for a suit o'
clothes and eleven-and-six."

" Eleven-and-six? " ses Sam, staring.

" Five bob for two hours' wait," ses the cabman, " four shillings for the drive here, and 'arf
a crown for the stable. That's fair, ain't it? "

Sam said it was — as soon as he was able to
speak—and then the cabman gave 'im a truss of
straw to lay on and a rug to cover 'im up with.
And then, calling 'imself a fool for being so ten-
der-'earted, he left Sam the lantern, and locked
the stable-door and went off.

It seemed like a 'orrid dream to Sam, and the
only thing that comforted 'im was the fact that he
felt much better. His illness seemed to 'ave gone,
and arter hunting round the stable to see whether
'e could find anything to eat, 'e pulled the rug over
him and went to sleep.

A Circular Tour

He was woke up at six o'clock in the morning by the cabman opening the door. There was a lovely smell o' hot tea from a tin he 'ad in one 'and, and a lovelier smell still from a plate o' bread and butter and bloaters in the other. Sam sniffed so 'ard that at last the cabman noticed it, and asked 'im whether he 'ad got a cold. When Sam explained he seemed to think a minute or two, and then 'e said that it was 'is breakfast, but Sam could 'ave it if 'e liked to make up the money to a pound.

"Take it or leave it," he ses, as Sam began to grumble.

Poor Sam was so 'ungry he took it, and it done him good. By the time he 'ad eaten it he felt as right as ninepence, and 'e took such a dislike to the cabman 'e could hardly be civil to 'im. And when the cabman spoke about the letter to Ginger Dick he spoke up and tried to bate 'im down to seven-and-six.

"You write that letter for a pound," ses the cabman, looking at 'im very fierce, " or else you can walk 'ome in your counterpane, with 'arf the boys in London follering you and trying to pull it off."

Sam rose 'im to seventeen-and-six, but it was all no good, and at last 'e wrote a letter to Ginger Dick, telling 'im to give the cabman a suit of clothes and a pound.

" And look sharp about it," he ses. " I shall expect 'em in 'arf an hour."

" You'll 'ave 'em, if you're lucky, when I come back to change 'orses at four o'clock," ses the cabman. " D'ye think I've got nothing to do but fuss about arter you? "

" Why not drive me back in the cab? " ses Sam.

" 'Cos I wasn't born yesterday," ses the cabman.

He winked at Sam, and then, whistling very cheerful, took his 'orse out and put it in the cab. He was so good-tempered that 'e got quite playful, and Sam 'ad to tell him that when 'e wanted to 'ave his legs tickled with a straw he'd let 'im know.

Some people can't take a 'int, and, as the cabman wouldn't be'ave 'imself, Sam walked into a shed that was handy and pulled the door to, and he stayed there until he 'eard 'im go back to the stable for 'is rug. It was only a yard or two from the shed to the cab, and, 'ardly thinking wot he was doing, Sam nipped out and got into it and sat huddled up on the floor.

He sat there holding 'is breath and not daring

to move until the cabman 'ad shut the gate and was driving off up the road, and then 'e got up on the seat and lolled back out of sight. The shops were just opening, the sun was shining, and Sam felt so well that 'e was thankful that 'e hadn't got to the horsepittle arter all.

The cab was going very slow, and two or three times the cabman 'arf pulled up and waved his whip at people wot he thought wanted a cab, but at last an old lady and gentleman, standing on the edge of the curb with a big bag, held up their 'ands to 'im. The cab pulled in to the curb, and the old gentleman 'ad just got hold of the door and was trying to open it when he caught sight of Sam.

" Why, you've got a fare," he ses.

" No, sir," ses the cabman.

" But I say you 'ave," ses the old gentleman.

The cabman climbed down off 'is box and looked in at the winder, and for over two minutes he couldn't speak a word. He just stood there looking at Sam and getting purpler and purpler about the face.

" Drive on, cabby," ses Sam. " Wot are you stopping for? "

The cabman tried to tell 'im, but just then a policeman came walking up to see wot was the matter, and 'e got on the box agin and drove off. Cabmen love policemen just about as much as cats love dogs, and he drove down two streets afore he stopped and got down agin to finish 'is remarks.

"Not so much talk, cabman," ses Sam, who was beginning to enjoy 'imself, "else I shall call the police."

"Are you coming out o' my cab?" ses the cab-man, "or 'ave I got to put you out?"

"You put me out!" ses Sam, who 'ad tied 'is clothes up with string while 'e was in the stable, and 'ad got his arms free.

The cabman looked at 'im 'elpless for a moment, and then he got up and drove off agin. At fust Sam thought 'e was going to drive back to the stable, and he clinched 'is teeth and made up 'is mind to 'ave a fight for it. Then he saw that 'e was really being driven 'ome, and at last the cab pulled up in the next street to 'is lodgings, and the cabman, asking a man to give an eye to his 'orse, walked on with the letter. He was back agin in a few minutes, and Sam could see by 'is face that something had 'appened.

"They ain't been 'ome all night," he ses, sulky-like.

"Well, I shall 'ave to send the money on to you,"

A Circular Tour

"So long."

ses Sam, in a off-hand way. "Unless you like to call for it."

"I'll call for it, matey," ses the cabman, with a kind smile, as he took 'old of his 'orse and led it up to Sam's lodgings. "I know I can trust you, but it'll save you trouble. But s'pose he's been on the drink and lost the money?"

Sam got out and made a dash for the door, which 'appened to be open. "It won't make no difference," he ses.

"No difference?" ses the cabman, staring.

"Not to you, I mean," ses Sam, shutting the door very slow. "So long."